PIRATE'S GOLD

ARGURMA SALVAGER BOOK 2

S.J. SANDERS

©2020 by Samantha Sanders
All rights reserved.

No part of this book may be reproduced or transmitted in any form or by any means, electronic or mechanical, including photocopying, recording, or by any information storage and retrieval system, without explicit permission granted in writing from the author.

Editor: LY Publishing
Cover Art: Sam Griffin

This book is a work of fiction intended for adult audiences only.

Intergalactic Files
Argurma Biology Data:
Access Granted

The Argurma species evolved as a skilled predator in their desert world of Argurma. Possessing inner secondary membranous eyelids, an internal purification system that allows them to filter their air and siphon out sand from expulsion areas beneath the jaw, and highly adaptive internal thermoregulation that allows them to remain cool in extreme heat, and to tolerate extreme temperature drops at night, they have evolved to survive hard conditions that would kill many other species.

Males and females stand within the same height range, although they show noticeable gender dimorphism with the presence of mammary glands and a paler crest of vibrissae on the females. The vibrissae are sensory receptors like in most species, but among the Argurma, they evolved to be thicker, with protective layers so that they resemble tentacles. They have a prehensile quality that allows them to vibrate and move in different ways, not only for gathering information, but also for defense and mating purposes.

When it comes to natural defenses, both males and females have hard scales everywhere, except the vulnerable areas around the belly and genitals, where they have soft flexible scales. Horns grow at several defensive areas on the body, protecting them sufficiently from many dangers, including predators. Although infants are born with soft scales and are more vulnerable until their juvenile scaling comes in around the third revolution, the species overall is difficult to kill with many weapons, which was the case even prior to technological advancements and the Argurma cybernetic revolution, which infused the species with tech implants and nano cybernetics, the full functions of which are still unknown.

The Argurma's ability to survive in varied terrain without protective gear, outside of those that are among the colder zones, also owes to the fact that the adults can go long periods without requiring food or water—a period of three weeks has been recorded in some extreme circumstances. While infants and juveniles require more regular feeding, their calorie needs decrease after reaching adulthood. Some adults will calorie load, however, if they know that they will not be able to eat for days at a time, in preparation for mating and in females when carrying young. A male Argurma will calorie load if he can twice a day when mated to assure that he has enough energy to care for and protect his mate.

On whole, it is the recommendation of the intergalactic survey team to suggest that the Argurma species, while possessing a keen intellect and strong forces that can be powerful in an ally, be avoided. It must be noted to especially avoid confrontations with mated Argurmas, and never get between a male and his mate.

PROLOGUE

Terri strode through the space station, trying not gawk. It was difficult not to. Everything was just so… *shiny!* After a lifetime of scraping by in shambles and filth, seeing so many new wares, flashy bright lights, and the scents of so many interesting things sparked an ember of avarice in her. She was greedy for it all! She wanted to taste, smell, touch, and experience everything.

She watched as credits were exchanged between flashing wrist comms and merchandise was bought. So that was what all Veral's fuss was about…credits. Credits acquired things. She was practically giddy with excitement as she took it all in. Males and females of peculiar species and varied appearances enticed her with colorful baubles and food that teased her senses.

A male waved around some sort of meat on a stick as he called out to those passing by him. Terri's stomach growled plaintively. It was torturous to stand among everything so tantalizing while Veral spoke to a male he apparently recognized. No doubt his contact for the furs he brought to trade. His head was lowered as he spoke in quiet tones, his dark form standing out against the brilliant colors of the hub. Terri didn't want to interrupt him, but she was *starving*. She didn't have any credits, and she felt a prick of guilt, but she wasn't going to let that stop her. She was hungry, and the male had more than plenty. Surely, he wouldn't miss one skewer. She would be quick—while the merchant in front of her was distracted.

She licked her lips, her muscles shifting as she prepared. She would be in and out before the male even knew what happened. She tensed and moved in for the kill.

Her foot slid forward on the floor when a hard hand closed around her shoulder. Her breath left her in a rush, emitting a slight squeak as Veral yanked her back against his abs, and she wheezed as her mate made a sound that was suspiciously close to a growl. Catching her breath, Terri leaned her head back against his hard body and met his piercing gaze, a slow, innocent smile spreading over her face.

"Done already?"

Veral rumbled, his vibrissae moving around his head with a bit more snap than its normally languid movements. His glowing eyes narrowed on her. "Did I not instruct you to not get into trouble?"

She gaped up at him. "I'm not in any kind of trouble. I was just here, observing all the interesting things in the—what did you call this place—a market?" She looked around once more, a heightened pleasure stirring in her breast as she took it all in.

Yes, she liked this place.

"If you steal, you will attract unpleasant attention," her mate growled out. "We are only here to make our delivery, not to draw unwanted notice to ourselves."

"I wasn't going to steal. I would never take what someone else needs to survive. Can't you see that the male has plenty to spare and is offering them indiscriminately to everyone who passes?"

"You know exactly how the credit system works," he replied

flatly. "We discussed it at length before our arrival on the space station."

He had gone over it until her eyes threatened to cross from boredom. Scavenging was a lot less complicated. You found it before someone else did, and if they had surplus that they failed to protect, then it was fair game.

"I'm hungry," she informed him irritably. She was always hungry as of late, her body demanding more and more nutrition.

"You are angry," he observed, his head cocking with curiosity as his perceptive gaze scanned her.

"Angry-hungry," she corrected.

In her mind, this was distinct. She wasn't really angry, just feeling particularly unreasonable while her belly wasn't satisfied. Though she was no stranger to going hungry, she found that she couldn't abide by it now that she knew what a full stomach felt like. A new situation demanded its own word.

"I'm hangry," she amended at last.

"*Hangry…*" Veral drawled, his brow plate lowering in consideration. "Is this something particular to your species? I have nothing on this in my databases."

Terri shrugged. Whether it was or not didn't particularly concern her. She just knew how she felt. She wanted to eat and felt more irritated every moment as her stomach gurgled and whined at her to be fed. If he wasn't going to allow her to procure it for herself, why wouldn't he just get her the damn food she needed? She glared at him impatiently.

A guttural sigh rattled out him, and he leaned down to press his lips against the top of her head, swaying his vibrissae to hide the gesture from prying eyes. His kind didn't kiss, but he was picking it up quickly and rarely hesitated to shower her with such affection when they were in private. Only in private. This was as close to a kiss as she was going to get outside of their quarters. In Veral's mind, kissing was akin to sex in intimacy.

The gesture still was comforting as his mandibles scraped through her hair a little and his hand smoothed over her belly. "Very well. I understand your irrational instinct. I will provide you with sustenance to sate your angry hunger momentarily. Be still while I finish my negotiations."

Terri grimaced and nodded her assent as she entertained herself by glaring holes through the merchant. The male seemed to be in no hurry, but dithered over the promised credits until Terri gritted her teeth so hard that they were on the verge of breaking. She could tell that Veral's patience was evaporating as well by the way his vibrissae began to move erratically.

Good. She wouldn't be wasting any sympathy on the merchant when he got a boot up the ass.

She was still glowering and had paced a couple feet away to look at a box of fascinating gems to keep her mind off her hunger when a trilling sound distracted her. Glancing up from the box, she found herself staring at a dull brownish-red creature with enormous yellow eyes, the one who'd been selling delicious meat sticks moments earlier. It no longer held tasty snacks. Instead, several tentacles unwound from its neck, moving toward her as the tentacles along its back and sides moved in.

Terri watched them warily, kicking away one in disgust when it got too close to her boot. What the fuck? She choked out a surprised gasp when a tentacle slithered up the back of her thigh, darting between her legs. Though she was wearing the black armored suit that Veral had fitted her with, she still squeezed her legs together in shock, gripping the tentacle with one hand, attempting to rip it away as it prodded at the strong material covering her sex. The tentacle dripped fluid from small tubes near the tip, and she felt sick as a substance like pale blue cum smeared over her gloved fingers, but still she couldn't dislodge it.

Gross!

She snarled and fought with it as other tentacles closed around her, the male drawing nearer. Another tentacle neared her face, and she sank her teeth into it. It tasted awful, and to her horror, the thing moaned rapturously and moved nearer, its tentacles reaching, stroking, and grasping.

An enraged roar made her attacker freeze. Veral's mandibles clicked threateningly as he pulled it away from her, dangling the creature in the air. The tentacle that had been prodding at her sex moments ago was gripped firmly in her mate's hand, his claws extended through the slits in his gloves. The alien squealed and attempted to break free, but Veral laughed as he held it in place.

"You dare to touch a mated female? *My* female?" he growled.

The alien shook its bulbous head. "I did not know—"

Veral snarled, shaking the alien in his grip.

"I am not ignorant of your kind. Male Manvi taste the air, seeking mated and unmated females alike guaranteed to be of breeding age to deposit your seed and breed when opportunity presents itself. Your mistake was daring with an Argurma's mate," he hissed, his mandibles widening aggressively.

The Manvi began to shriek as Veral's claws dug into his mating tentacle, tearing into the flesh as he twisted and pulled on the limb until it tore free, blue blood spurting everywhere. His screams were so terrible that they drowned out the panicked shouts of the merchants fumbling as they searched for a safe place to hide.

Terri watched as the blood splattered on Veral, but he didn't appear to notice it. His teeth bared in a savage grin, he transferred his iron grip to the male's jaws, forcing them apart, and silenced his screams by shoving the tentacle deep into the gaping mouth.

Her assailant made a ghastly gurgling sound as Veral finally dropped him and turned nonchalantly to greet a group of males. They were dressed alike, and each possessed an air of authority. She determined that they must be the space station guards her mate hadn't wanted to attract the attention of.

Wiping a bit of blood off her cheek, she stepped on the Manvi, grinding her heel as hard as she could into the place where the tentacle was torn free, and wandered over to his stall. Without hesitating, she helped herself to several meat sticks, loading her arms with tasty treats. Sinking her teeth into one and ripping away a deliciously spicy chunk of meat, she returned to Veral's side.

One of the uniformed males was grimacing down at the Manvi. "You are fortunate that the species breathes through a low set of gills over their chest or else we would have no choice but to bring you up on attempted murder charges," he muttered.

Veral shrugged. "I would not have cared if he died, but I am familiar with the species and know the laws."

The male nodded, his eyes sliding over to Terri and her pile of snacks—more specifically eyeing the food. She clutched them defensively to her chest and glared. If they thought they were going to take them away from her after she been assaulted and with her belly complaining, they were going to have to wrestle them away. The male's eyes narrowed as if debating doing just that until Veral growled. Not wanting to cause an altercation, Terri smiled cheerfully and waved a stick.

"I think after everything I just had to go through, sacrificing his dignity and a few snack sticks is an appropriate payment."

The male, never taking his eyes away from her growling mate, nodded slowly and cleared his throat. "Yes, I can see how that would be reasonable. What is your business on the Xenxinexa space station?"

Veral's vibrissae twitched as his mandibles clicked with impatience. "Our business is between us and our employer, a respectable merchant on Xenxinexa."

The guard's eyes sharpened as if weighing whether or not he wanted to pursue the matter. The Manvi gurgled again, and he grimaced down at the poor wretch. "This is going to take considerable time to write up," he huffed at last. "You and your female are free to go. I trust that you are not planning an extended stay with us."

"No," Veral grunted, grabbing her arm as he turned away. "Our business is concluded. We are leaving."

Terri was certain she heard a muttered prayer of thanks as her mate hustled her away, back toward their ship. His eyes cut to her, softening in amusement as she gnawed eagerly on her treat.

"Are you still 'hangry,' anastha?"

She licked the spices and delicious flavoring off her lips. "I think I'm good. How did business go?"

Veral grinned as he fingered his comm unit. "The male rethought his bid and doubled the original offer."

"Wonderful!" she said. "Before or after you threatened his life?"

Veral smirked and curled a protective arm around her. "It may depend on who you ask. According to my processors I had not yet threatened, only suggested what happened to males who cheat an Argurma."

Terri chuckled as she pressed her cheek lovingly into his side. "I love you."

"This I know—which is very fortunate for the other males in the space station staring at you, stinking up their air with their lust."

Grinning widely, Terri fed a bite of meat to her mate as she bit off another chunk, chewing happily, Veral's raspy chuffing surrounding her as they entered their ship.

Despite his good humor, her mate gave her a sideways glance as they settled into their chairs on the flight deck, his expression turning thoughtful.

"It may be prudent if you stay aboard the ship next time. The males exhibit too much interest in you. I do not mind exercising my right to protect you and detach their reproductive organs from their bodies, but it unnecessarily alarms security and brings attention on us."

Terri frowned at him in confusion. "I don't see how it is my fault."

Her mate's expression softened, a soft purr vibrating from him. "It is not your fault, anastha, that you attract the attention of males. But I do not wish for my female to be in danger."

"But how am I in any danger with you at my side?"

She had her answer three days later when a group of vaguely familiar males trailed them from the space station and attacked. Veral allowed them to dock and slaughtered each male who attempted to board their ship. Their screams had echoed through the ship into the quarters she shared with Veral, making her hands tighten into fists against the bedding.

She understood the danger then, but she didn't think he would follow through with his plan.

Terri didn't even think of it when they received an assignment from the Royal House of Grezna to salvage a load that had gone down when the starship carrying it crashed. Although it had been weeks since the incident, and Terri herself had almost forgotten his quiet decision, when they stopped again to take on more fuel, Veral had kept to his word and locked her on the ship for her safety. Bewildered, she waited for him, and he returned with their supplies.

Each time they stopped as they passed through the quadrants, she was left aboard. It was only then, after the third stop, that she realized just how serious he had been about protecting her.

1

Four Months Later

Stars surrounded the ship in an endless field, one that changed only minimally as they traveled through space. Oh, the placement of the stars did shift as they flew from one quadrant to another, but to someone who knew dick about space, it all started to blur together in an unending, unvarying nothingness. They were now on month four of their journey to salvage in an outer alliance system, and it felt like they would never get there.

Terri held back a sigh. There were some impressive sights to be seen, but only if she happened to be on the flight deck, looking out of the viewing screen at the right time. It wasn't as if the male she mated a few months ago ever alerted her to anything new they were coming across unless it was to tell her to brace for impact, or to hide when someone was hailing his ship.

It was only a couple months ago that just being in space had still been a fascinating adventure to her. It was preferable to the dying world that she had grown up on. When she left the planet with the alien salvager, Veral, she had been excited about what the universe held. Unfortunately, the adventure had already dried up when it became apparent that the male was not only overly protective but territorial to the point that she never got to do anything.

After an unpleasant incident with a male trader the first—and only—time she had been on a space station, she was left locked on the ship with Krono, the enormous canid-like dorashnal, whenever Veral had to disembark. There was a vague promise that she would be able to get out when they got a salvage assignment, but this was the first one that had come up.

His worry was understandable. She got it. Being on the space station just once made one thing really clear to them: with the human species nearly gone and almost unheard of in space, and Terri likely the only one of her species who left Earth, it made her exotic and coveted. She hated it.

After dealing with the gangs on Earth who gleefully kidnapped women, she hadn't considered that in space she would be dealing with the same issues. Unfortunately, even the slightest interest in her direction drove her overprotective mate murderous. She didn't pity those who had tracked and attempted to board their ship only days after leaving the space station. As far as she was concerned, they got what they deserved, but it did suck that it resulted in Veral being paranoid about anyone even knowing that she was onboard.

Terri shifted in the seat he had installed near his and glanced at her mate's profile. The vibrissae that hung from his head like numerous thin, black tentacles made a whispering hiss from their tiny rattlers as they moved around his shoulders. It still amazed her that the huge alien beside her was her mate. Every inch of him was lethal to the core, his cybernetics glowing under his skin adding to the impression, especially when knowing that his cultural norm was to be "advanced" enough that emotional impulses that overrode the cybernetic codes were considered a defect.

She didn't want to complain of how bored she otherwise was, not when she had changed his life the moment that they mate bonded. All his work to control his emotional impulses so that he wasn't branded as defective had gone out the window when the intense emotions of the bond had left him helpless to hide them. He knew that his affection, love, and even jealousy—all things she greedily enjoyed—were a death sentence. Because of that, he had given her the choice to stay on Earth.

She could have lived her life in safety in the sanctuary city, but she chose to be with her mate. She willingly chose this life with him. She didn't regret it—there was really nothing for her on Earth—but she did worry that her decision to accompany him had made his attempts to avoid his people all the more difficult.

He refused to speak of it when she attempted to bring it up, but it had become an uncomfortable point between them. Everything was fine as long as she didn't mention it, but it didn't stop her from thinking about it constantly as of late. Even in plotting out their course to check out wreckage on another planet, she had noted that Veral had gone out of his way to burn extra fuel to avoid inhabited zones.

All because of her.

She wasn't stupid. She knew that eventually they would see more bounty hunters from Argurumal. They already had two who came after them on Earth, and Veral was certain that it was just the beginning. She also knew that he was worried about it, even if he didn't share his concerns with her. The only thing he allowed himself to vent his grievances about were the males whenever they encroached anywhere near their ship. Though he hated other aliens' attempts to steal her, he didn't truly worry about them. Much of his venting was an outlet for his true concern: his people tracking them down. The salvager was their only refuge, and it wasn't exactly secretive when they depended on taking odd jobs.

At least this time she would get to do some actual salvage work, and she was going to be on a planet! Sure, they made a stop to retrieve furs for an employer, but Veral had insisted she stay inside due to the number of unmated males approaching their ship... and that was before the space station incident. This time, since they were salvaging alone, she would be able to get out. She grinned at the idea of getting to stretch her legs on an alien world. If only they could just speed up the travel time. She'd assumed that they would be there in a matter of days—not months.

"You are restless, anastha," Veral observed, his mandibles making a soft clicking sound as he examined a schematic blown up on one corner of the viewing screen.

Terri hid a frown. She hadn't meant to be so obvious.

"I am just eager to get started on our salvager," she corrected with a small smile.

His eyes turned toward her and narrowed, his mandibles letting out a sharper click. Although her mate wasn't particularly expressive unless under the influence of strong passion or rage, she had come to notice the subtle nuance of his "you're full of shit" expression.

"Honestly! Okay," she conceded after he kept staring. "I may be feeling a bit impatient. I guess I didn't realize just how long it would take."

A soft chuff erupted from her mate, his glowing blue eyes warming by degrees.

"Is this not what I told you? There are great distances that have to be traveled when salvaging."

"I know," she grumbled. "I just didn't think it would be *that* long. Plus I didn't get to leave the ship with you when you last refueled and restocked our supplies, so it feels like it's stretching on forever. How many more days are we estimating here, anyway?"

She frowned at the way Veral's vibrissae quivered in amusement, his lips tugging upward. Her face flushed with embarrassment as she shot him a mild, chastising scowl. It was bad enough that she verged on whining—not that it wasn't a legitimate observation—but now he was laughing at her.

"Time estimation: eight days until we are in orbit of outpost planet Tignr."

She cocked her head. "Outpost planet? Does that mean there are people there?"

Veral shook his head, his vibrissae swinging with the movement. "Negative. The outpost planet is on the edge of the Megnax system and could serve as a defensive base if threat ever broached that part of the system."

"So why haven't they sent someone out before now? Why contact us if it's within their own system?"

That alone confused her. From what Veral had told her, professional salvagers were typically employed to retrieve property when it was either too far away or too dangerous to retrieve themselves.

Veral clicked thoughtfully. "The planet is far enough away from their regular trade routes that it is more cost efficient to hire a salvager, especially when retrieving valuable cargo in a potentially hostile environment. A professional salvager is trained to work within parameters that include unknown factors. The royal house is paying well due to these factors." He paused and hissed. "Recent scans transmitted reveal that the ship is estimated to have gone down over area comprised of dense foliage." He frowned. "Unfortunate."

Terri's eyebrows rose. "Why? Do you have something against plants? It sounds like a nice change from the brutal conditions of the desert."

"It is illogical to suggest that I bear ill-will toward plants," he scoffed with another chuff. "If you look at the schematics, you can see the issue. Thick plant life indicates the presence of ample amounts of water, which can be problematic with equipment. We will not be able to take the collection units in with us. Thick plant life will not only conceal the wreckage but hamper any recovery. It would have been better if the ship had crashed in the arid band just above the jungle, or in the wasteland zones."

She couldn't say that he was wrong, but she also wasn't going to pretend like she wasn't happy that they were going somewhere green. Instead, she made a noncommittal sound in her throat as she leaned forward, studying the schematic. As best as she could make sense of it, anyhow. Some of the information she still couldn't quite make heads or tails of despite Veral's best efforts.

She was grateful that her mate was teaching her to read the various symbols and markings, but it was slow going and she wasn't retaining it well. It was maddening! Terri always considered herself reasonably intelligent, and yet she struggled with many of the basics that were common knowledge among the spacefaring races. Her mate's unflagging patience didn't make her feel any better. In fact, it made her feel like a useless drain of resources every time he had to reteach her something. She comforted herself that at least she had a broad sense of the topography, even if many of the details were still vague.

Eyeing the schematic of the planet, her attention was drawn to a squared off coastal section that was almost smack in the center of the tropical band.

"That marked area—that's where we're going, right?"

"Correct," Veral replied as he enlarged the area.

Several deep gullies were marked out bordering a long inlet from the sea. She pursed her lips. Ravines could make access a bit more challenging than she was imagining. And the water was plentiful as Veral said.

She licked her lips. "Uh, what are the chances of it being *in* the water?"

Tromping through shallow water she could handle. Anything more significant...

"Odds of submersion with the water and landmass ratio of the area is approximately sixty-five percent."

"Oh, fuck. Please don't let it be submerged," she prayed to whoever was listening. "I can't swim, and this would be a really bad time for a crash course."

Veral grunted, his mandibles quivering slightly, just enough to betray his unease. "It would not be ideal. Argurmas are made to sail over deserts, not to swim," he muttered.

She raised an eyebrow at him, her curiosity piqued. "Do you know how to swim?"

"The mechanics of it—yes, I have that information. I also have experience in the practical application of those mechanics to propel myself through water when necessary. My ability, however, is unsatisfactory."

"So if I start drowning, don't look to you to save my life," she said. "Got it."

His head whipped to her, an affronted snarl rumbling in his throat. "I would not allow any harm to come to my mate and offspring. My ability is adequate enough to secure your safety."

Terri laughed, her hands raised in surrender as her mate vocalized as an exasperated click from his throat, far louder than the subtle sounds made by his mandibles.

"Your humor is questionable, anastha," he growled, returning his attention to the viewing screen.

A frown pulled at his mouth as he downsized the schematic and enlarged a pulsing mark on their navigation board in the opposite corner. His lips peeled back into a frustrated growl.

"To our quarters. Immediately," he ordered brusquely as he pushed up from his chair to stride across the deck.

Terri bit her lip. She was once again being sent to her room like useless baggage. "Veral, maybe there's something I can do to h—"

"To our quarters!" he barked out, his vibrissae rattling as they snapped through the air. They gradually slowed as he focused on her dismayed expression. He swallowed and glanced back at the alert on the navigation board. When he spoke again, his voice was measured once more, though carrying a note of concern. "Anastha, you must return to our quarters... and quickly."

"We're supposed to be in this together. Partners and mates, helping each other," she reminded him softly.

"This is true, and right now you will serve your part by following my directions. An unknown vessel approaches, and I will not chance any harm coming to you. You know where the blaster is. Your job presently is to protect our offspring should anyone board the ship and attempt to harm you."

He regarded her firmly for a moment before turning once more to his controls, giving his full focus there. She waited, watching him, hoping he might call her back to remain by his side to face this unknown. Any hope that he might fled as his vibrissae began to stir once more in agitation. Kronos looked up from where he lay against one wall and whined, the cluster of vibrissae around his head moving alertly.

Pressing her lips together, Terri nodded and left the flight deck with Krono following close on her heels.

2

Veral narrowed his eyes on the approaching vessel. For the last several minutes, he had been ignoring the comm request from it as his mate made her way to their quarters. He knew she was unhappy with his decision to send her away, and her impatience and restlessness were becoming increasingly more apparent, but it was what was necessary.

He did not trust anyone when it came to her safety. Least of all those who send out emergency hails in the vast stretches of space between habitable planets so close to the system's fringes.

Linking into his ship's systems, he tracked Terri as she made her way toward their room at the well-fortified heart of the vessel. Strictly speaking, it wasn't the official captain's quarters on the salvager. That was a large room that stretched across the entire front of the vessel beneath the protective shelter of the flight deck. It had once been luxurious, with a vast viewing screen.

When Veral took over the ship, however, being a reasonable and cautious male, he calculated the chances of damage done during an attack even with the protection of the flight deck and found it unsuitable. It had not taken him long to convert three of the smaller crew quarters that went unused near the center along a narrow corridor into one large chamber, and he turned the other room into a storage and work area. It had served him well over the years, and now with a mate on board the past several galactic standard months, he could not think of a safer place for his female.

Autolocking the door behind her, he withdrew his consciousness from the ship and accessed his comm system.

"Open frequency. Respond to hail," he ordered.

The system complied, and the viewscreen in front of him opened a window that filled the surface with the frowning countenance of the Blaithari. The delicately scaled pink male regarded him hesitantly through gold eyes before bowing and bringing all six of his palms up in supplication, the scarlet crests of his hair arranged in six knots bobbing as he moved. Veral curled his lip at the copious amounts of jewelry dripping from the male. The male was a fool to comm a stranger who might rob him. Even the robe he wore was of the finest quality that spoke of wealth of a station or prestige.

Either a very wealthy trader or a male of a noble house from Blaitharsha.

Veral's mandibles clicked as he returned the Blaithari's regard suspiciously. "This is Salvager Vessel 289-Veral. What assistance do you require?" he growled ungraciously.

He could almost sense his mate's disapproving glance at his immediate hostility and repressed a smile. Terri was a soft-hearted female. She did not understand the necessity and thrill of instilling fear into one before they got it into their heads to do something unwise.

The Blaithari cleared his throat nervously. "Greetings, Salvager Veral. I thank you most graciously on behalf of Oulia and Motang, the benefactors of..."

"These details and thanks are unnecessary," Veral interrupted, his vibrissae twitching more aggressively around him. "What assistance do you require?"

"Yes, of course... I... that is...I, Egbor of House Torg'bornor formally request emergency transport to Zarcruga."

"No. I will transport you to Janilik. It will put me two days off schedule, but it is within my means."

Egbor gaped. "But that is not where I need to go! I am to settle into an agreement on Zarcruga, not Janilik. I am already behind schedule."

"Then get on your long-range comm and find someone else to assist you," Veral replied coldly. "Zarcruga is behind me, and I do not have the time or inclination to backtrack many days to transport you. You can repair your ship and continue on to Zarcruga from Janilik. Your business on Zarcruga is no concern of mine."

The male looked around at the males nearest him as if seeking some support. Veral's lips quirked as he took note that not one of them took their master's side against him. The male wilted as he faced Veral once more.

"We are left with no choice. Our life support systems barely have enough power and are in rapid decline. We do not have the power to send a long-rage comm. It is only fortunate that we managed to bring our ship to a stop when the thrusters went offline rather than sail beyond the regular trade routes. There are only five of us who require lodgings upon your ship..."

"No!" Veral snarled, his vibrissae instinctively moving so viciously that the male in the screen stared at him with stunned horror. Although it was near useless since the male was not close enough to get further readings on, the overall result through the comm was at least satisfying.

He would permit no strangers upon his ship!

"But... our life support. We only have a few galactic standard hours left at most before it is completely gone. The ship is already miserably cold with the failing systems. How would you expect us to survive?"

Veral hissed in frustration. He wanted to tell the male that his capability for sustaining life was not his responsibility... but he also knew that Terri would not approve if he let the male freeze to death or asphyxiate when the life support failed. There was a good chance that she might not find out. Yet there was an equal probability that she would learn of it. If she learned of it, she would be extremely displeased that someone actually died. Maybe if he tried to explain to her that it was for her safety...

"Salvager, I really must insist..." the male interrupted, his chest puffing out in a show of bravado before his crew.

Veral glared at the male. "I am considering my options. Be silent."

"Options?" the noble squeaked. He instantly deflated, his gold eyes widening to a ridiculous proportion.

Veral's mandibles opened wide and returned to their resting position as he turned the matter over in his mind. He was aware of the way the male seemed to watch every movement.

No. Terri would not accept any excuse for the deaths of the Blaithari. He would have to allow them to board.

Rules. There would be many rules.

"Very well," he snarled, his mandibles snapping loud enough to make every male in the viewscreen jump. "Prepare to dock with the salvager. Once you enter the cargo hold, do not venture into the ship without permission. I will meet with you there shortly."

"Yes, of course," the male said quickly.

Veral did not wait for any other needless conversation. He terminated the comm signal and left the flight deck. The Blaitharis could wait until after he spoke to Terri. She was not going to like what he was about to propose.

It took him considerably less time than his mate to stride

down the corridors to their room, his mind interfacing with the ship to unlock the doors minutes before his arrival. They slid open at his approach, and Veral purred as his mate looked up from where she lay stretched over the bed. She wore soft, loose clothes that clung to every curve, the line of her breast enticing him. His purr became louder, and Terri's brows drew up as she trailed a teasing hand down her belly. Although he did not arrive with copulation on his mind, his desire surged to the fore at the sight that greeted him.

Aggression stirred within him at the thought of the males close by—too close to his private dwelling where he and his mate slept. He was filled with an instinctive drive to fill the ship with the stink of their pheromones so the males had no doubt as to whose territory they were in.

"What happened?" Terri asked, her voice soft with concern.

"Stranded travelers," he grunted as he drew nearer to her.

Dropping down onto the bed beside her, he nuzzled her soft hair, his vibrissae twining through the strands. A hand stole up her belly, brushing her fingers out of his path as he leaned into his mate, his desire roaring. His civix—or cock as his mate called it—strained against its fleshy pouch, eager to be released. It took so little for his small mate to stoke his passions.

Terri captured his wandering hand and frowned. "That wasn't very long ago. Where are they?"

"Waiting in the cargo hold," he replied as he leaned down to stroke both of his long tongues down into the waistband of the pants she wore, his nose nudging lower.

"Oh, okay, good," she rasped as his tongues found the soft, hot little place between her thighs. He growled at the taste of his mate, and then snarled as she jerked out from underneath him. "Wait... They're in the cargo hold, the one you don't bother to heat since we don't transport livestock—*that* cargo hold?"

Veral growled, his sex straining impatiently. "I increased the heat to livable levels. They will not die before I arrive."

"We are not fucking while you just leave them waiting on you," she snapped as she moved out from beneath him. "That's just weird."

Though he hissed with frustration, he drew up from the bed reluctantly. He had no house to give for her to rule, as was the custom of the Argurma, but still, he would follow her lead on issues pertaining to their home and family. If she insisted on immediate hospitality toward their "guests," then he would see to it as long as it did not interfere with her safety.

His instinctive impulse to cover the ship in fresh layers of his scent would have to be ignored.

Pushing himself from the bed, he stalked toward the door. He froze, however, when he saw that Terri was following close behind. Stopping in front of the door, he turned toward her, his arms crossed over his chest.

"It is necessary to discuss rules before I leave."

"Rules?" she asked, her nose wrinkling in confusion.

"Yes, rules. Over the course of the four-day journey to Janilik, you will keep to our quarters as much as possible. If you need to be out in the ship, you will wear the shafna. The robe is large enough to conceal most of you. Be certain to keep the hood up and to not get close to any of them. And keep the door locked. Do not answer to anyone. They will be able to scent your presence on the ship, and I do not trust them to not attempt to gain entry to the room."

Terri mimicked his pose, her own arms drawing across her chest. "I guess that I wait here while you go to the hold? And lucky me, I get to stay here for the rest of the day as well. I hope they plan on paying us for our hospitality if I'm getting locked in our room."

He drew his hand against her hair, down to cup her cheek in

his palm. "I will be sure to exact a fair price for the inconvenience. Do not be angered, anastha. It is for your safety. You are too precious for me to dare to risk."

Her pale brown eyes softened, and she sighed. "Oh, all right, I'll wait here. I'm not going to be happy about it, but I will stay."

"Krono will keep you company."

Her lips quirked. "That's a given. I think sometimes you find Krono a more dependable barrier than the door."

A smile pulled at his own mouth. She was not wrong. Brushing his lips and mandibles against her brow, he exited the room, once more securing the locks behind him. At least his stop at his quarters served a purpose. He was once again calm.

Or so he thought, until he entered the cargo hold. Rage rattled through him as he observed Egbor sniffing at the air, his pink scales flushed brilliant red with the sexual interest that sullied his cargo hold. Cold, hard fury slammed through Veral as a snarl escaped his throat, his vibrissae rattling menacingly around him. The male was so caught up in Terri's scent that he did not seem to notice. Instead, he moaned with delight.

"This scent! You have a female on board—a most exquisite one. I will double any credits you require if you allow me to honor you by requesting her company during our travel."

Veral stared at the male, his muscles quivering with restrained anger.

"Honor… me…?" he asked, menace dripping from each word.

"Oh, yes, it is considered an honor when an heir of a noble house requests the company of a commoner's mate. It is not only our right per our divine lineage, but it blesses their home with great fecundity. I would be most happy to bestow this blessing. In fact, my galari is eager to impart its duties. If you will just show me to my chamber and escort her…"

Drawing back his fist, Veral restrained himself enough only to knock the male unconscious. He wanted to do far more damage, but with the way the other males cowered around their fallen noble, he considered well enough done. His mandibles clicked in anger. *And she wonders why I keep her away from other males.* Everything about her was exotic and unknown. It unfailingly attracted the wrong kind of attention. He would not tolerate the disrespect being shown toward her. Not by space station vermin, and not by foul nobles flaunting their privilege and wealth.

No one was going to touch his anastha.

"Pick that thing up," he snapped at them, gratified when they complied.

Within minutes, he had the entire group secured within two of the crew cabins with strict instructions when it came to what parts of the corridor were off limits. The males bobbed their heads in quick agreement. He had no doubt that they would follow orders. His eyes narrowed on the unconscious male before pointing one claw at his prone form.

"Keep that male away from my quarters and my mate or I will make certain that his galari cannot bless another female again," he growled.

Without another word, he stalked from the room, his vibrissae snapping around him with hissing rattles as he prowled back toward the flight deck.

The sooner he offloaded his "guests," the less likely he would kill Egbor.

He smiled at the thought of the male's blood and entrails falling from his fingers and allowed himself to enjoy the visual for a moment before banishing it to the recesses of his mind. As long as the male followed his directions, that would never happen. The males accompanying the noble better pray that their leader was not so foolish.

3

Veral did not trust the males. His hands came down on the controls as he watched them shuffling through the corridors of his ship. Although they stayed well away from the quarters he shared with his mate, these *guests* were being far too free with his ship. When he had approached Egbor about it, with a demand that it stop, the infuriating male had shrugged and said that Blaithari required regular exercise and he would not be sequestered in his room like livestock.

Veral seethed with the analogy, unable to stop from comparing the statement to his mate's own miserable confinement. It made him bristle even more, his vibrissae churning around him, taking in the male's exact distance to effectively strike as he made his displeasure known.

This ship was property of his mate by Argurma tradition. *She* should be wandering through it freely. Not them.

He bristled as one of the males sniffed curiously in the hall just as the door to the flight deck slid open. Turning a disgusted look on Egbor as the pompous male leisurely strolled in, Veral huffed and returned his full attention to the male in the security vid running behind his eyes.

"I have never been in a salvaging ship before," the male announced politely as he narrowed his eyes at one of the downsized schematics.

Veral whisked it away with a thought and frowned at the male. He did not find curiosity to be a virtue or tolerable in most individuals. Where it was delightful in his mate, in everyone else, he found it intrusive.

"What do you want?" Veral demanded.

"Want? Nothing at all. It is so taxing remaining in my quarters all the time, as you know, and I had not yet seen this part of the ship… and now here I am. So tell me, what additions does a salvaging ship have compared to other spacecrafts?"

"None," Veral replied, willing to tell the male what he wanted to know if it would get rid of him. "It can be modified to haul ships when necessary, but the ship itself is a means of transportation with an upgraded reinforcement. The strength of a salvage is dependent on the training of those doing the work."

"On the salvagers themselves? Oh my, that does sound taxing, but certainly puts things into perspective as to why males of your skills are so valuable." His lips pursed thoughtfully. "How much longer until we arrive at Janilik?"

"Eighteen standard galactic hours," Veral grumbled.

It could not be soon enough for his comfort.

Egbor sighed. "I do not suppose you can increase your speed? I am running very late. This delay is inconvenient enough as it is."

"The ship is going at maximum drive speed. Anything faster could not be maintained for long distances without potential damage to the ship."

"I could compensate you generously for the costs…"

"No," Veral snarled, terminating the conversation with that one word.

"You really are a most disagreeable male. Is this typical of your species, or do you strive to be unpleasant and difficult in general?"

"The Argurma do not care what outsiders think, so we make no special effort to be either agreeable or disagreeable," Veral said coolly before flashing the male a hard smile, baring his sharp teeth in a manner that disturbed most other beings. "That you find it personally offensive is merely a detail that I individually savor."

"Well," the Blaithari huffed indignantly, "I shall retire to my quarters then with a cup of orshan tea."

Veral curled his lip but did not reply. Instead, he watched the male, tracking him with his eyes as well as the vids throughout the ship as the Blaithari flounced back to his quarters. He stopped at the corridor junction to stare down toward the room where Terri was hidden before resuming his irritated pace of the remaining distance to his quarters. Moments later, one of his attendants scurried out to the galley, filling plates and replicating a pot of tea that he hastened back to his master's quarters.

Though he watched for considerable time, the males did not emerge again until a single attendant rushed back to the galley with the dishes to wash and store for the next meal period. After the conclusion of their meal, he noted that one would slip out every so often to pace up and down the corridors. They often took breaks to stare out the viewing ports scattered along their route, and they never failed to miss the port just within the junction that led to Terri.

There was a certain purposeful stillness to them as they looked out the ports that Veral did not like. It was as if they were intentionally positioning themselves at regular intervals close to his mate as if he would not notice if repeated. If that was their intent, they failed. Instead of shrugging off the repeated behavior, it made him increasingly anxious of the distance between himself and his mate.

Unable to stand the torment of separation a moment longer,

his entire body vibrating with territorial aggression, he left the flight deck. His mandibles clicked and a low growl churned continuously in his throat. He hoped to meet with one of the males as he made his way to his quarters. He would relish the opportunity to strike terror of promised pain upon them. Unfortunately, the male who had been lingering at the junction returned his master's quarters moments before Veral arrived. His eyes narrowed at their noted absence before striding into his cabin, his vibrissae hissing around him.

Terri looked up from where she was sprawled across their bed with a datapad clenched in her hands. Her eyebrows winged up. As he stood there, his eyes fastened on his female, his entire body wound tight with aggression.

There was no fear within his little mate, however. As he stalked toward her, he scented her desire bloom and ripen as he drew closer. The protective menace he projected seduced his mate and sharpened her arousal almost as much as it would have done had she been Argurma. He needed that acceptance while the whole of him burned to mark his mate thoroughly. Her breath came out in a sharp gasp of pleasure when he stopped just in front of her only to reach down and grip her thighs. With one smooth move, he lifted her up and tossed her gently further back on the bed.

He did not wait to follow. With a press of his finger twice in rapid successions against the high collar of his suit, it promptly split open and slid off his body to pool at his feet. Stepping free of his suit, his civix stirred and slid free from his genital pouch. The long shaft writhed and twisted eagerly as the hooked head sought his mate's entrance, the narrow tubes running up its length dripping with a steady flow of lubricant.

Veral's back bowed as he fisted his civix with a rough snarl. Eyes dragging back up to his mate's expectant gaze, he climbed over her body eagerly. His female was equally aroused, and she held her arms out for him, her thighs opening to accept the girth of his heavily muscled body.

As his hands and vibrissae skimmed over her, he drank in the flush of her skin and the heat of desire in her arms. His civix coiled against the lush petals of her sex and Terri hissed, her hips jerking up against him. A needy sound escaped her throat, but he stroked himself over the mouth of her cunt, allowing his fluids to coat and smear against the flesh, working his pheromones deeper into her skin until finally, with a driving snap of his civix, the head buried deep within her, the small hook brushing against her sensitive spots.

Terri's cry filled his ear as he pressed his face against hers, his mandibles sliding open wide to brush possessively against her throat, grazing the sensitive skin there. In reaction, his mate trembled, her sex reflexively squeezing around his as he snarled and fought against her grip with ecstatic jerks of his civix within her.

Every time the sensitive hook brushed against and became gently caught in the soft, wet grip of her channel, it made his testicles draw tighter and a tiny spurt of seed escape as a small orgasm swept through him. Every gentle tug against his sex as he thrust powerfully into her, his civix writhing, driving in and out of her, tightened the pressure within him. His body shook, and he stroked his tongues against her shoulder, needing just a little more.

He needed everything from his female.

His testicles drew up tight again, and with a hiss, he tore from her body only long enough to flip her over onto her belly. His claws latching onto her hips, he made a loud growl of pleasure when she responded by lifting her ass up higher, presenting the wet, dripping folds of her cunt open for him. He buried himself within her once again, his grunts and pants joining her soft gasps and moans.

He felt the ripples of her sex caressing him, drawing him in deeper, squeezing his civix. He felt the hook extend just enough so that it clung to the soft, spongy tissue at the mouth of her womb. The sensation tugged from deep within him at the same moment that his mate convulsed, her cunt gripping him as she screamed, sending him barreling into his own climax that ripped out as a ragged roar from his throat.

Shifting them to their side, Veral curled around her, satisfaction thrumming through him at the fresh scenting on his mate. His vibrissae curled over her skin possessively, assuring him that she was sated. It was a small comfort, but he would take it. His vibrissae coiled around her shoulders in a protective shroud, covering her breasts in swathes of dark, twisting tendrils. Even still, it was not enough to settle his unease.

Terri's fingers came up and stroked along the vibrissae in a light, soothing motion. "Feel better now?"

"No," he grumbled.

"What can I do to help make it better?" she teased.

"You can give your consent for me to jettison them all out of the airlock," he hissed.

Her body shook against his, the brush of it stirring him all over again despite having sated himself moments earlier within her tight, hot cunt. The fact that she was laughing did nothing at all to cool his passion. Terri pushed away just enough to turn in his arms to face him. She eyed him as she continued to stroke his vibrissae.

"Have they done something that bad?"

"No," he growled. That was the point. He didn't want them to attempt to.

Terri sighed and tucked her body in closer against him in a manner that he found soothing. It had not taken his mate long to find the best ways to calm him. Her voice was low and gentle as she continued to speak.

"I know they frustrate you, and impede on your space, but

we're halfway to Janilik. Let's not kill our guests when we're so close to finishing," she said.

"That male walks on my ship as if it is within his command," he protested.

"I hate to point out that you do that everywhere," she said, laughter evident in her voice.

He narrowed his eyes on his mate but purred contentedly, a reluctant smile pulling at his mouth. His mate was not wrong. Argurma were raised to see all the universe as potentially theirs by the strength of their discipline and the might of their cybernetically enhanced bodies. They held back from expanding through the cosmos due to a distaste for other species and a desire to remain insular within their own quadrant of space.

Unable to deny her observation, he grunted, his arms tightening around her small body. Her limbs and body had thickened to a healthier state after a few standard lunar cycles passed. She was still tiny compared to his species and most others out there, but no matter how large or small she was, it did not matter. She was entirely his. He needed nothing else. That said, the ship was hers—and he was tired of these males encroaching on his mate's space.

"You should permit me to jettison them. It will give me some pleasure to be free of them and allow my mate to walk her own ship in peace."

"*My* ship?" she asked, eyebrows raised.

He chuffed at her surprised expression. "I have told you. Argurma females are the right of lineage and the property owners. Upon our mating, all my belongings become yours, except those which are most personal and necessary for my wellbeing as a warrior."

She shifted against him excitedly. "That means I can name her."

He frowned down at Terri. "Name the ship? It does not need a name. It is a serial number. That is adequate identification for a starship."

Terri rolled her eyes at him. "That's boring, and I can never remember that random spew of numbers. Don't worry. Leave it to me. I'll think of something good."

She lay there beside him, tapping her fingertip to her chin as she began listing absurd names, each one more terrible than the last.

"How can you not like *The Screaming Lady*?" she protested after the tenth suggestion, her fingers tracing the scales on his chest. "We both know that when we don't have company, there's a lot of screaming that goes on in here. It would be a very good name."

Veral did not miss the sexual reference and curled his fingers around her questing hand. "No. As much truth as your observation contains, the name is undignified."

"So you want a dignified name, then?"

"I do."

"Okay. I'll give it some thought," she said with a long-suffering sigh that made his lips quirk.

"Now that is settled, about the airlock—"

"No!" Terri laughed as she smacked him ineffectively with a pillow.

Snarling, Veral curled over his mate, pressing her small body into the bedding. His muscles trembled, eager to attempt to convince her otherwise. As his civix slid into her hot clutch, he groaned. He rocked into her with abandon, her soft sighs and moans mixing with his growls until they both shouted their completion again and again.

Though her answer did not change, they both enjoyed his attempts to alter them. He looked forward to trying to convince her many more times over the next eighteen standard hours.

4

*M*ade of a thick, durable material used by Argurma when they had to move across vast deserts on their homeworld, the shafna was always uncomfortable. Although Veral hadn't been home in years, the first time he had Terri wear it, he had been pleased that he kept the enormous hooded overcoat. She could have done without it, but since it allowed her to leave their room despite the company on board, she couldn't hate it too much. Especially not with the bright gems that their passengers had been carrying, samples of a larger collection being gifted to the Grez'na prince for his betrothal—whatever the hell that was. The word was used in some of the older books from Earth, but she didn't know what it meant. All the same, having to wear it when she wanted to leave their quarters was a good enough deterrent to keep her away from the strangers.

Until now.

Three days in their cabin and Terri felt like she was on the verge of going mad staring at the same four walls. During the day, Krono kept her company, curled up at the foot of the bed, only to be released to prowl the corridors so that Veral could slide into bed next to her at night. At first, she had worried that one of the

Blaithari would be hurt by the protective dorashnal. When she voiced her concerns to Veral, he had smirked without sympathy but assured her that their guests knew not to leave their quarters during the night cycle. He even set an alarm that went out over the ship every night at the start of the cycle so that everyone knew to return to their cabins.

Not that Krono was entirely cooperative about the matter, as accustomed as he was to being with them at all times. He was eager to scout through the ship when Veral first returned to the room, but they were both woken at ungodly hours as the animal attempted to break back into the room, not once but multiple times. The sounds were both monstrous and pitiful, but after a while, when Veral made it clear he wasn't letting the dorashnal in, Krono trailed off to find something else to occupy himself with until morning.

Though she felt bad for Krono, Terri appreciated that Veral didn't just hover on the flight deck the entire time as she half-expected him to do. It was a huge concession when she knew that the presence of the strangers on the ship drove his protective instincts wild.

She understood, but enough was enough. She couldn't spend another moment trapped in the room all day. She needed to get out, and besides—she'd been craving! There hadn't been any cravings in the initial months of her pregnancy, but she had been struck by such an intense need for *something* that, when it didn't go away, she had to search it out.

She was *so* damned hungry!

Terri knew he wouldn't approve of her slipping out during midday, but she was still following his rules. She tugged the hood on and smiled down at Krono, who stared up at her, his mouth gaping in an expectant dorashnal grin, his vibrissae relaxed against his neck as he watched her for any cues.

"Shall we go play with the replicator, Krono?" she asked her companion.

His mouth gaped wider, and he whined with excitement. He was fully on board.

Humming under her breath, Terri headed for the galley. Slipping inside, she stilled as she watched the two pink Blaithari standing with their heads bent in close, whispering as they filled their trays and a third. Their nostrils suddenly flared and both heads came up and turned toward her, gold eyes gleaming.

Terri felt a jump in her belly at the intense way they were staring at her. She would have run right back out of the room if she hadn't reminded herself that she was wearing robes. Of course they would be curious. Veral had informed her that he circulated a story among them that she was horribly scarred from a cargo fire so that they wouldn't be suspicious if they happened to see her. Still, it did little to settle her nerves as she gave them a polite nod to acknowledge their presence before scampering by them.

Both males immediately backed away, their eyes darting down to Krono, who stared at them, his ears turned alertly in their direction.

Watching them out of the corner of her eye, she frowned at how massive the aliens were. From Veral's description, she was expecting small, slender males, not ones who were—despite being close to the height of an average human male—packed solid with muscle. Granted, they likely looked small and unthreatening to a male Veral's size.

They were clothed in beautiful swathes of fabric, but as they slipped by her, she couldn't hold back the shiver of dread that ran through her. They looked at her just a little too carefully, a little too long for her comfort.

She turned her gaze back down to Krono to find him still staring at the empty doorway, his vibrissae whipping around him. His head angled up to stare back at her, and she let out a small sigh. Dropping her hand to the top of his head, she scratched him behind the ears and smiled.

"Just nerves, that's all," she whispered. "Now let's get something to eat."

Terri stared at the food replicator, uncertain of what she wanted. She grimaced at some of the selections as she scanned through the holo-menu. Agami worms, steamed tirichi—a large beetle-like insect—in a mendak egg sauce. She gagged as she bypassed a large selection of Argurma delicacies. No insects... Hell no. She may have been hard up enough on Earth to survive on a regular diet of reptiles, but she couldn't stomach eating insects.

Finally, she came to the wrapped scourra and sighed gratefully. Scourra was a livestock animal that tasted a lot like what she imagined beef once did. She didn't know for sure, outside of a few questionable old cans of beef stew, but it was close. There was also a kind of noodle made of some sort vegetable smothered in a rich, spicy, nutty sauce. She licked her lips, making a few more selections as she scrolled through. There was no way in hell she was going to be able to eat all that... Maybe. It just all sounded so good, and she wanted all of it. Her pregnancy seemed to make the sharp bite of hunger felt more keenly.

Plates full of replicated food, and even a bowl of peeled slices of the foul axna fruit at her elbow, filled the small table in the galley. She eyed the spread as her stomach rumbled again. It felt like she had a huge hole where her stomach was. Perhaps pregnancy cravings weren't going to be so bad. If only she could figure out just what it was that she was wanting.

Sitting at the table, she dutifully choked down the slices of axna and then dug in, the spices incredible as she plopped every morsel in her mouth. The nutty noodles and some strange fatty meat in a sauce that tasted something like the wild chilis she would occasionally find around Phoenix made her wiggle in her seat with joy as she stuffed her stomach. But what really satisfied her craving were the crispy-sweet nuggets. She wasn't sure what they were, but they were both spicy and sweet all at once, and she loved them. When she bit into them, they oozed a sticky sweetness that made her tongue curl with delight.

"Anastha, you should have commed me if you hungered," Veral growled.

Terri looked up and met her mate's glittering gaze with a grin.

"Last time I 'hungered' when it was day cycle, you told me very specifically that you were not leaving the males run of the ship to satisfy our urges. So I decided to take care of it myself," she replied as she glanced down his broad, muscular body, licking the bit of sauce clinging to her lips a little suggestively.

Veral growled again, his eyes narrowing on her, the tiny circuitry under his skin flaring brighter with the all too familiar spark that ran through him.

"You know exactly of which hunger I speak. This hunger I could have seen to without concern. You should have commed me and told me what you needed. I would have brought it to our quarters."

Terri shrugged and mopped up a bit of sauce with a fragrant hard bread that, like the noodles, had a bit of a nutty taste. Not that she was one to judge. The only nuts she ever ate were some really stale peanuts she found as a kid while digging through a collapsed section of what had once been a grocery store. The taste was vaguely similar.

"I didn't know what I wanted. I think this is the pregnancy cravings all the books I've been reading talked about."

"Cravings?" Veral paused, his head cocking as his eyes ran over her.

She nodded her head. "Yep. There's a book in that huge collection you downloaded into our system called *What to Expect When You are Expecting*. I figured a lot of it would probably be as useless as a fishing pole in a sea of sand since this baby is half-Argurma, but it did talk about some of the things I would experience as a mom, like morning sickness—thank fuck I've managed to pass on that so far—and food cravings. I really wanted to eat something, but I had no idea what. So here I am. These, by the way, are just the thing."

She tossed a handful of the sweet crisps into her mouth and groaned aloud at the taste once more lighting up her tongue.

Veral's eyes flashed with humor, his lips quirking. "You enjoy vansik?"

The way he said it had her pausing, the sweet morsel at the edge of her lips as she looked at his suspiciously. He knew her food phobias and found them highly entertaining. That he was amused about her pleasure when it came to eating vansik wasn't a good sign.

"If you're about to tell me something disgusting, keep it to yourself. This is one of those times where I don't want to know and will kill you if you ruin this for me."

He shrugged, his vibrissae twitching over his shoulders as he watched her place the vansik on her tongue and slurp into her mouth. "I just thought my anastha had an aversion to eating insects. No insects, no bodily organs, nothing made of boiled or fried blood… you have an unreasonable list."

Terri felt her face pale as the sweet innards dripped over her tongue. "Insect?"

"You did not wish to know, so I will not tell you," he said as he sat beside her and began to snatch food up with his claws.

She glared at him and shoved several more vansik in her mouth. Fuck him. They tasted good.

"I don't give a fuck. They're good."

"I am glad you think so," he replied mellowly. "They are an acquired taste on Argurumal. Some like the sweetness, but few can get past that they are round parasites that live in large colonies in the liver of the igwinpek—sandshark, I believe you would call it. It is similar to the shark in your planet's wildlife catalogs except that it dwells in the sand dunes and has two powerful legs for when it needs to surface above the sand. The vansik bloat themselves on the heavy sugars in the igwinpek's blood. When they are cooked over intense heat, the sugar-rich organs liquify."

His eyes fastened on her as he finished his explanation. She knew he was getting some satisfaction from the entire situation considering how many times she gagged and made rude comments about his love of tirichi. But that was different. That literally looked like an enormous beetle laid out, half-circled in on itself and covered in sauce. The smell of dead bug had been just enough to make her want to hurl. The vansik didn't look or smell like anything she recognized. As long as she didn't think about it, she would be fine.

Stubbornly, she lifted a handful and threw them into her mouth, letting the sweet round bits burst as she chewed them. Veral chuffed with humor and leaned forward, his two slender tongues snaking out to swipe a drop of sweetness from the corner of her mouth. She flinched, heat flaring to life in her belly as he regarded her, his face inches from her.

"As it so happens, I very much enjoy vansik. I do not think I have tasted it sweeter, however, than from my female's mouth."

With that, his mandibles spread wide enough to just graze the sides of her cheeks as his mouth claimed hers. The press of his hot lips sparked something within her. His tongue swept into her mouth, drawing along her tongue and licking at the insides of her mouth until she squirmed with pleasure. He froze, his muscles tightening and his tongue retreating as the sound of a blaster priming filled the air.

"As much as I hate to break up this sweet moment—on your knees, Argurma," a voice said coldly.

Terri looked up, and she too froze. The Blaithari were no longer in fine robes, their hair gathered into crude knots rather than fussy styles that Veral described. All three males held blasters pointed directly at them. A rattling growl hissed out from between Veral's lips, increasing in volume as he turned toward them, his inky vibrissae whipping around his dark silver face. Despite his obvious anger, he dropped to his knees, his muscles straining with tension.

The male at the fore, who could only be Egbor, nodded toward her. "Retrieve his mate and bring her over here. She is the tool with which we will control him."

Terri balked as one of the males drew up beside her. Krono snarled and the male promptly shot the dorashnal, dropping him to the floor. A scream tore from her throat, and her mate whipped around, but stilled when the male set his plasma pistol at the side of her head.

"Do not do anything stupid," Egbor snorted. "The animal is currently stunned so that it can be safely caged. I would rather not kill until I am required to make my point. It is a messy business… and besides, the animal can be sold for a considerable amount of credits. Bring her here, Irgnar."

The growl grew more vicious, which prompted Egbor to smile down at him. "Do not worry. I will not be touching your mate, not unless I have to. This is far more effective of an arrangement. You do what you are told, and your mate suffers no harm."

"Do not come between an Argurma and what is his," Veral warned.

"Oh, I know. If it were not for the fact that I am in need of a skilled salvager, I would have chosen an easier target. But as it happens, I require your particular skillset."

"This was a trap," Terri whispered in horror.

Egbor turned toward her, his expression curious as he yanked back her hood. His brows raised, a red flush streaking through his scales.

"Well, I see why you hide her. Terrible scarring from a fire was a good ploy. So exotic. There are of course worse fates that death for a specimen such as this. I could sell her or give her over to my crew. There are all kinds of possibilities that you have within your power to avoid. And yes, little female, it was a trap. One that we have employed many times and has served us well. But hearing of a great treasure to be found on the *Evandra*... well..." He left the words hanging as he shrugged with a hard smile.

Cheerfully, he wagged his pistol toward the door. "I do believe it is time to dock with my ship. Your proximity alerts should be detecting its presence—" An alarm trilled, and his smile widened. "Now."

With a dark glare, Veral rose to his feet and allowed himself to be led to the flight deck with Terri hauled between the two lackeys at the rear. Any attempt to twist away was met with a tightening, painful grip on her arms until she stopped. They half-dragged her through the corridor after her mate, her feet barely able to keep up with their long strides.

Mentally, she cursed the men holding her, relishing the thought of when Veral would tear them apart. The thought withered and died when she entered the flight deck and got a look at what exactly they were facing. Terri's eyes widened at the enormous gray ship that filled the viewing screen. It had to be crewed by hundreds.

Her mouth went dry. They were so fucked.

5

Vibrissae rattling, Veral stalked through the flight deck, the three Blaithari trailing close behind him, holding his mate captive. *Pirates!* His mandibles clicked with self-disgust. The traveling noble disguise had been a clever ploy and was executed convincingly. He never would have guessed that they were anything other than what they said, their sickening, privileged behavior the one thing that successfully persuaded him to avoid their company. Not even on the vids at any time had they broken character. It had been flawless.

Still, he should have suspected something—anything.

There had been no cues that he picked up on. Instead, he had been enraged at their presence and offended by their presumption. He had even pressed his engines as hard as he dared, despite his words to Egbor, with the goal of arriving at Janilik earlier than planned.

He had been right, although for entirely different reasons. He should have thrown them out of the airlock.

At the nudge of the weapon firmly at his back, Veral stiffened and cast a concerned glance at the males crowding close to him. Terri's face was pale with fear, but when she met his eyes, he could see the spark of anger in their amber depths. Her eyes lifted away from him and returned to the viewing screen, and her lips thinned.

He wanted to tell her not to look at it and assure her that he would get them to safety. His desire warred with the practical side of him that sneered at the sentiment and demanded to know just how and when he was planning on doing so. The pirate ship filling the viewing screen carried a large crew to successfully pilot it. He could kill Egbor, but if he did, the other males would kill Terri before he had the opportunity to reach her.

Even if he managed to save her, the ship's systems alerted him to the fact that the pirate vessel was locked on to them. He had no choice but to bide his time and wait for the most opportune moment to strike.

Egbor waved his blaster lazily toward the control panel, belying the sharp focus of his gaze as he grinned. "Begin docking procedures, Argurma."

With a clicking growl, Veral approached the display to manually to put in the codes. The male obviously did not realize that Argurma warriors had the ability to sync to their vessels. Veral did not need to touch the control panel to begin the sequence, but he would not enlighten the male otherwise. That ignorance worked to his benefit. For once, he wished that he was less scrupulous, like his cousin Kaylar, who entertained himself with creating virus codes to infect enemy ships.

He hated to involve his cousin. No doubt the male would have heard of the bounty and could be tempted to turn Veral in to claim it. That possibility was not something he could concern himself with that at that time. As much as he hated it, he needed Kaylar's help to keep Terri safe. That the Blaithari pirates knew nothing of Argurma implants assured him that at very least he could get a message out on their private family frequency. His cousin would have the means to disable the pirate ship. All Veral needed to do was stall the pirates and wait.

"Perhaps Argurma are as intelligent as everyone says. Cold logic, rather than passionately trying to rip your female away. Very good. Now upload the schematics into my comm uplink." With one hand pointing his blaster still, he stepped over to the uplink port and attached his comm with a sharp jerk of his hand.

Veral suppressed an agitated growl as his ship's systems established the link. Egbor's tech felt invasive and filthy to him. An unwanted intruder. Stealing a quick glance at his mate's face, her expression twisted with anger. Despite the flare of fear in her eyes, he maintained control over his reaction. Instead, he met Egbor's eyes and, with a flick of his finger on the control, sent the schematics outlining the ship's resting place over to the pirate. The male grunted in satisfaction, the hum of the engines as the salvager ship drew into the cavernous mouth of the pirate ship the only other sound.

He was uncomfortably aware of Terri's hard, nervous exhales as the darkness engulfed them. They were dragged into a docking area that was pitch dark when the hatch closed. Once it snapped shut, so many lights shot on that it blinded him. At Terri's cry, he looked over at her, concern rising within him as she screwed her face up, her eyes clenched shut. The pain and disorientation were intentional. Veral closed his inner lid, filtering out the worst of the light until, as predicted, it dimmed to a more comfortable level. Only then did he lift his inner lid to glower at his surroundings.

From the viewing screen, he could see a number of pirates from the less savory dregs of space milling around. None of them were anywhere near as well dressed as Egbor. In fact, many of them wore tattered, ill-fitting clothes that might have once been fine before being soiled with blood, food, and sweat. Igwin males with long jointed limbs prowled, large heads swiveling and mouths stretching in wide grins as they paced like beasts waiting to be fed.

While there were many Igwins, they were not as numerous as the Blaithari and the Turogo, a vile, squat race that lived in their primitive swamps. Pirates recruited among them, promising them treasures, taking advantage of the males' drive to collect gems and gold with which to line their muddy hollows in hope of attracting mates. What they lacked in intelligence they made up for in thick, muscular bodies and venomous teeth and claws. Even their long tails could loop around another being to squeeze the life out of them.

Veral growled and attempted to place his body directly between them and his mate as they were forced to disembark into the belly of the pirate ship. It did little good as Egbor made certain to keep him separated from his mate. Veral's vibrissae rattled in a warning hiss as he snarled and clicked his mandibles in clear threat at any male who so much as looked his mate's direction. A threat was all it amounted to, and the males knew it, but it did give some among them pause.

Egbor opened his arms wide, a satisfied smile on his face as he addressed the crew. "Miscreants, look at what your own captain has secured for the benefit of all of us: a way to find the resting place of *Evandra*."

A riotous shout drove up all around them, males raising their weapons in the air in a frenzied jubilation. Numerous swords and axes clanged together, and blasters fired into the air. With a shove, Egbor drove him forward, but Veral stalled, his attention always on his mate behind him. Her body jerked in alarm as the Igwins sniffed, licking their jowls as they raised their short muzzles to scent the air, and Turogos uncoiled long tongues from their mouths which they flicked at her without any discretion, stealing small tastes of her skin.

Her captors allowed Terri to bat away the tongues with angry squeaks of disgust because they found it amusing, but did nothing to protect her. Crude, hard, scraping laughter surrounded them, their shouts of delight rising among the cacophony of banging weapons at every flinch from Terri. She was brave in face of the slavering interest of the males pressing in around them, but she did not have complete control over her natural reactions. Nor did he.

As an Argurma male, he was accustomed to possessing exact control over so many of his reactions, but he had no control when it came to his mate's distress. Every dismayed sound she made enraged Veral, his fury mounting with every step deeper into the belly of the pirate ship.

Eventually, they arrived at the brig. It reeked of old blood, urine, and rotten food. An aged door swung open to reveal a cramped cell with nothing inside except a thin, dirty mat thrown on the floor against the wall and a rusted container to expel wastes in tucked into the corner. The cell was so small that there was barely enough room for him to stand in front of the bed as he allowed himself to be herded into the cell. Just as he turned around, the cell door snapped shut, securing him within.

Vibrissae whipping, Veral charged forward, his body slamming into the bars of the door, shaking the entire construct. Unfortunately, everything was well secured, and it didn't give when his body collided with it. That didn't stop him from wrapping his fingers around the bars and attempting to rip it free from where it was bolted. His mandibles clacked as he hissed at Egbor, who regarded him smugly from the other side. Terri remained wedged between the males just behind him.

They were going to keep her separated from him!

Egbor's smile widened. "Do not worry. Your mate will be well taken care of. You understand, of course, that I cannot allow you to keep her in here with you. Not when she is the key to maintaining your cooperation."

Eyes narrowing on the male, Veral's lip curled back from his teeth as he lowered his head and brought his face closer to the bars to meet the Blaithari's gaze. "If any harm comes to her, you will beg me to end your life. Know this: I will show no mercy and every plea will fall on deaf ears. Control me if you must while you can, but be certain that no harm befalls my female."

The male stared back at him thoughtfully, his head tilted in consideration. Egbor's nostrils flared, and his shrewd gaze took in every lethal inch of Veral's killing expression directed at the Blaithari.

A low chuckle rolled from Egbor but he inclined his head in agreement. "I like you, Argurma. It is rare that I meet a male who is nearly as bloodthirsty as me. You would have made an outstanding pirate. Very well. I shall give you my personal guarantee that your female will not come to any harm. She will even have her own quarters, well-guarded from any unseemly conduct from my crude crew. You just keep doing what you are doing—you will lead me to the ship."

Veral jerked his chin toward Terri. "If you intend to take her planetside, she will need the suit provided for her on my ship in cargo bay. She will require the extra protection, as small and delicate as she is."

The Blaithari waved a claw absently. "Yes, yes. I would have figured as much. I will send one of my trusted males to fetch them for her before we make planetside."

"I want her untouched," Veral hissed. "If you guarantee that no one will lay a hand or civix on her, then I shall not feel inclined to remove them. There will be no other male's scent upon my mate."

The captain frowned. "You drive a hard bargain."

Veral snarled at him. He did not care. He would do nothing unless his mate's protection was guaranteed in all ways.

Egbor narrowed his eyes. "If I make this concession—and it is a significant one for a female so rare and exotic—then you will lead us faithfully to the resting place of the *Evandra*?" He crossed two pairs of his six arms, his right hand of the upper set drawing up to tap his bottom lip thoughtfully, weighing his options.

Veral did not like giving the male what he wanted, nor losing the credits and cycles spent on the salvage already—but he would do anything for his anastha. He jerked his head in a stubborn nod, and the male clapped his hands, crowing with delight.

"Excellent!" Egbor trilled. "Very well. You have my word." The male paused and narrowed his eyes in a cold assessment. "But just so we are clear, since you were so honest and in a sharing sort of mood when it came to what you would like to do to me… betray me and I will skin your female and feed every bloody chunk of her flesh to the Igwins after I have let them take turns in fucking her into a useless pile of flesh. Do we have an understanding?"

Sickness pooled in Veral's belly as he glared at the captain, his mate's gasp loud in the silence of the brig. Slowly, he inclined his head, and the captain's pleased laughter floated around him.

He opened his eyes and watched as Terri was pulled away. She kept turning in their grasp, attempting to keep him within the field of her vision, struggling against their hold to join him. He met her eyes and shook his head. She stilled, her face stricken. For the first time, he wished that she had the implants that his people possessed. He would have already had a private channel established to communicate with her.

Instead, he was forced to plead with his eyes.

Do nothing. Just wait and watch. Wait for the opportune moment.

She studied his expression as she was pulled toward the exit. Just before she was pulled through the doorway, she gave one short dip of her head. She had caught something, some small part of his intention. He hoped it was enough.

Her absence from the room drained his energy and spirit. With a roar he fell to his knees, shuddering with despair from the forced separation. A piercing pain filled him as if something vital was torn out from within him. His mandibles spread as he let loose another roar and another, his voice echoing through the brig as he vented his fury and pain.

6

Terri struggled between the Blaithari as they carried her caged between them, jerking her with each of their uneven steps as they entered the lift. At one point, she wondered if they were intentionally trying to pull her arms out of their sockets, as hard as they seemed to tug her between them. Despite the discomfort, she infinitely preferred their company to the other pirates who watched her every step through the pirate ship.

To her surprise, she saw few other Blaithari once they left the brig. For some reason, she had figured that that the captain would have arranged a crew primarily of his own species, but that didn't seem to be the case. Aside from her escorts, Terri only saw three or four other Blaithari during her trip to the upper decks where she was presumably going to be kept. For the number of males she had seen in the docking bay, it didn't make sense that there weren't more traveling to the upper level quarters. Not only was the short corridor empty, but of all the doors that lined the hall, all but two appeared to be sealed.

"I will be putting you in the room typically reserved for my second-in-command—if I had permitted him to enjoy it instead of housing him with the other upper crew members on the floor just below this one. I like my privacy… and I like silence," he stated, eyeing her sternly. "You should be comfortable in here so long as I do not hear any noise and you don't make any attempts to escape and make me regret providing it for you. It is the most convenient way to keep you away from my crew, but if you cannot behave, I will send you down to keep my upper crew company. I can trust them to follow my orders not to touch you, but the experience will be far less than pleasant."

So that was the way of it. She saw no other Blaithari because the captain kept the entire upper deck for his own use. No doubt the other males were crowded into the levels that they passed on the lift. It was clear that Egbor saw everyone as his lesser. Terri, as a member of another species, wouldn't have even the smallest amount of mercy from him.

All that kept him in check was Veral's promise.

Swallowing, Terri nodded to demonstrate that she understood exactly what her position was just seconds before she was dropped to her feet. She was pleased that she didn't stumble, despite how heavy her legs felt from being hauled through the ship by her arms. She did, however, straighten her back and meet the captain's gaze unwaveringly. It was a shame that he was no longer the sniveling, pompous male who Veral was complaining about only yesterday. The cold eyes of a killer stared right back at her, though his lips curved slightly at her show of bravado. She knew that he was aware of the conflict brewing within her.

As much as she wanted to tell the captain to go suck the biggest dick on the ship, she wasn't stupid. Since she couldn't join her mate in his cell, staying in this cabin was her only real option. The last thing she wanted was to be at the mercy of crew members who would do the barest to toe the line of whatever orders were issued by the captain. There was a lot of flexibility in regard to what lengths of unpleasantness they could get away with before the captain deemed it crossing the line. That meant that she would have to play by the captain's rules, however much she hated it. It was better than option two.

Sweeping one arm out, Egbor pressed his hand on a panel and opened the door. At the same time, his lower hand closed around her arm and yanked her forward, ahead of him, into the room. Terri stumbled forward a few steps but drew to a stop as she stared at her surroundings. Although possessing simple lines and sparse furnishings, everything in the room was far more luxurious than anything she had ever seen before. Compared to the filth of the rest of the ship, this was surprising. Her mouth hung open at the polished desk that sat in one corner as the captain steered her toward a chair and sat her down on it.

Leaning forward, his nostrils flared as he met her gaze with a steely regard. "I have been utilizing this room as my personal office. Be aware that all the drawers are keyed to me. You will not get anything out of my desk, and if you damage it by attempting to break into it… well, it has been passed down through my family for generations and I will find a way of taking its value out of your hide. Your mate was fond of rules. Here are some rules for you, and I suggest you heed them well. Rule one: do not try to leave this room. You are locked in, but do not get it into your head to attempt to escape in any clever method that may occur to you. You will fail and only bring my wrath down upon you. Rule two: as I said before, I expect silence. Any attempts to disturb my rest will be dealt with harshly. Rule three: I do not know what condition your species lives in on your homeworld, but you will not soil or otherwise destroy this room. There is a waste receptacle. I expect it to be used."

He straightened and smiled. "Now, I suggest that you rest. I will send someone to collect you to join me for evening meal."

"I would rather not," she muttered before she could stop herself.

His retaliation with immediate. A red-flushed hand swept

down to curl around the neckline of her shirt as he lifted her nearly off her feet. Only her toes just barely had contact with the floor when he leaned down and growled threateningly in her face.

"It was not a request. I will see you fed and guarded. You can at very least provide me some amusement during the evening meal. If you enjoy eating, I suggest that you do so. If you refuse to eat with me, then you will not be eating at all. It is still several diurnal cycles until we arrive planetside, where you might have an opportunity to forage."

"Is that rule four?" she squeaked. Her mouth was suffering from such a disconnect with her brain that must have had a death wish.

His nostrils flared again, but he smiled and dropped her back down into the chair. "Indeed. Rule four."

He reached out a hand as he stared down at her. One of his goons stepped forward and handed him a cleansing cloth. Egbor's eyes narrowed on her as he wiped each of his hands off as if he had touched something filthy.

She tamped down the offense that immediately sprung forward. No. It was a good thing if he thought of her as an unclean burden. She didn't want him to have any interest in her outside of how he might use her to manipulate Veral.

"Be sure to use the cleansing unit before you join me for evening meal. You will forgive me if I do not trust the hygiene of a salvager and his primitive mate." He snorted to himself in amusement. "I will send someone in with proper items for a female."

She would have asked him how a pirate ship had anything suitable for a woman, but he walked away without another word. Despite her gnawing curiosity, she didn't call after him. Instead, her body sagged with relief when the door closed behind him. From the chair, she allowed her gaze to wander. It didn't take long before she became restless enough to start poking around her surroundings. Just as he promised, everything on the desk was locked, as well as a nearby cabinet.

She had only just started really exploring the room as she tossed a couple of drawers filled with spare clothing and random items of no value to her when the door opened again to reveal at brilliant orange Blaithari. The female's four breasts were small but visible beneath her tight uniform, her dark hair pulled into a high knot at the back of her head, the remaining length trailing down her back. Her eyes were a very pale yellow, almost colorless, as they regarded Terri with icy detachment.

"The captain had me bring these things for you, female," she rasped.

The rough sound of her voice was so at odds with almost musical tones of the other Blaithari that it startled Terri, drawing her attention to the female's face. The Blaithari grimaced under inspection, her throat working as she choked back whatever retort she was going to fire at Terri's head. It was then that a thick network of scars lacing the female's throat were clearly visible.

"Quite staring, beast," she snarled as she foisted a bag into Terri's arm. "These are for your use. Be grateful. It is far more than any other would receive as captive on board *The Black Star*."

Returning her attention to the other female's face, away from the scars, Terri clutched the bag to her chest. "Thank you, uh…"

The female snorted rudely and squinted at her. "Azan. I suppose that you need to know it since Egbor is making me responsible for your welfare. Never known him to care so much about the comfort of a female in his life," she scoffed. "You must be something special… A rare pet? A princess? Yours is a peculiarly ugly species if you are. No scales, thin hair and nails, flat teeth, dull eyes, and only one set of arms and tits. I do not understand the attraction. Though I imagine you are warm and soft, which may be pleasing enough," she acknowledged. "I suppose that would make you an entertaining enough female for the time being."

Terri's eyes widened when understanding hit. "Oh no, there's nothing like that going on here. He is using me as leverage against my mate. The deal was that he had to keep me safe from the crew and this was his best bet."

"Was it now?" Azan murmured, her lips curving into a menacing smile. "*This* is hardly safe. I do not like being ordered to watch over you and see to your needs as if I were a servant. I have worked hard and sacrificed much to be second-in-command. That my sex has assigned me as your keeper is beneath me, as is being forced to share my meager belongings just because I am the only female on ship who has them. But," she said slowly with resignation, "the captain has entrusted me with this, so I will carry out his orders, regardless of my personal feelings on the matter. I only offer one warning: do not even consider doing anything stupid that may reflect poorly upon me."

Her words dropped to a whisper as she reached out and drew one claw along Terri's cheek. "I know ways to bring about pain. Pain is my special calling and is what secured my position in this crew rather than becoming of the few miserable females who live short, brutal lives, flung among the lower decks to amuse the males. I will find a way to inflict the worst pain on you without leaving a visible mark. While you are in my charge, you will do as you are told. It is as simple as that."

Azan made a show of relaxing as she straightened and rocked back on her heels. She glanced around the room placidly, a room that would have been hers if the captain assigned rooms in accordance to the ship's design. Her expression, however, didn't waver. It remained cool as she smirked at Terri.

"With arrangements as they are, I am going to be spending a lot of time in this room with you. If you don't like sharing a bed, you can sleep on the floor. I have spent enough revolutions on a floor that I refuse to go there again. Unless I am called away or need to step out for a specific reason, consider me your shadow. Now, I do believe that you have an evening meal to prepare for. Cleanse yourself and rest. Egbor is not a patient or forgiving male."

Shooing Terri off in the direction of the cleaning unit, Azan dropped down into the chair that she had vacated and pulled out a large, wicked knife and a small square block upon which she began to sharpen it. Terri watched, her heart hammering in her throat at every long draw of the blade against the stone. Azan glanced up and smirked.

"Hurry now, beast."

Biting off her protest, Terri spun away and disappeared into the cleansing unit. Her clothing hit the floor, and she stepped into the stall. The dry air and sonic vibrations surrounded her, stripping away every bit of dirt and sweat until she was as clean as she had ever been. Although she and Veral did have a tub for the rare occasion when they chose to use the recycled water supply for that, she had long become accustomed to a cleansing stall.

When she stepped out, she nearly tripped when she found the Blaithari waiting outside the stall with folded clothes in hand. Her eyes swept over Terri, and she grinned.

"Just as I suspected, you are wholly soft and helpless. You don't even have the lower pectoral spines."

"The w-what?" Terri sputtered.

The female pulled up her tight tunic just enough to reveal her breasts. Just as they were bared, a long, sharp spine speared up from beneath the swell of each breast before slowly retracting. Terri gaped in astonishment as Azan tugged her tunic back down.

"Most females have some sort of defense mechanism to protect themselves from aggressors—except your species, it seems. You are truly as fragile as you appear. You will not last a full revolution without your mate protecting you. I am surprised you have survived as long as you have. Soft things do not last long in space. How sad to see a male of such a strong species mated to one so weak. Argurma females are warriors who stand beside their males. He must have to keep you protected like a youngling."

With those parting words, she tossed the clothing at Terri and strode away, leaving Terri alone with her thoughts and the dread curling in her stomach. Obviously, Veral had known something that everyone in space understood but her. Anything perceived as weak wouldn't survive. On Earth, she was good at hiding from her enemies, but even she understood the need to fight for survival. If her survival meant that she had to go further to protect herself, then she would find a way to equip herself.

Terri's brow furrowed thoughtfully as she pulled the loose tunic and leggings on, all of which were baggy and obviously meant to fit the Blaithari who gave them to her. Her exploratory field armor in the ship was a good start, but she was going to need more, as Azan had made clear with her demonstration. She was letting Terri know with few words why her chances of survival were slim—and exactly why Veral jealously guarded her and kept her hidden away.

How long would she have survived otherwise? Especially with her penchant for finding trouble and aim to turn a quick profit. It would have earned her more than a little undesired attention if things had continued as they were with Terri so vulnerable.

Her teeth sank into her bottom lip. She needed to find a way to reduce her vulnerability so she would be able to survive this situation and be able to stand at Veral's side as his mate. But how?

7

When Azan escorted Terri into the captain's quarters for the evening meal, she found herself stepping into a room bedecked with precious metals and exotic, colorful fabrics. A sort of light, spicy fragrance hung in the air, though it was almost drowned out by the savory foods set out on several platters on the table at which Egbor sat.

Although she balked for only a moment, it was apparently too long for Azan. The second-in-command pushed her forward, giving Terri little choice but to sit in the chair directly across from him. The pirate captain regarded her contemplatively through slitted eyes. His eyes left her only long enough to acknowledge the presence of Azan as she took her place between them. Almost on cue, a thin male—a young Blaithari if Terri wasn't mistaken, not more than a child—drew to the side of the table and began to serve them in a careful, measured manner before scurrying out the door.

She drew back startled. "I really don't think…"

"Good. Do not think," Egbor interrupted, his expression hard.

She glared back at him. To her disgust, her stomach grumbled as the aroma of the food on her plate hit her nose. It was a wonder that she could eat, but her body was demanding the nutrients and letting her know.

A small smile tugged at the captain's lips as his expression suddenly lightened, and he gestured to her plate. "Despite what you may think from your current surroundings, we do not stand on ceremony here. Eat."

She did not reply other than to grab the two-pronged utensil sitting beside her and dig into her food. She felt a pang of guilt as the tender meat melted on her tongue. There was little doubt that Veral wasn't getting anything this good. She cut a quick glance to Azan, and seeing her engrossed in her own meal, she ventured to broach the topic.

"Did anyone bring food to my mate?" she inquired cautiously.

Egbor paused, his two-pronged fork halfway to his mouth as he stared at her. "Yes," he answered shortly before placing it in his mouth. He chewed as he regarded her. "He is being given a portion of what was sent to my upper crew. Nothing quite as fine as this, naturally. In fact, Azan hasn't enjoyed such fare herself in many revolutions, but he will still have food of filling and good quality. The Argurma is a fine tool, and I will care for him as long as he continues being useful to me."

Terri stared at him in surprise. "But you put him that a tiny, dirty cell."

"That is to remind him of his place and his dependence on my good graces. In any case, it will not hurt him. Argurma are resilient. He will care more about the food than he will about a comfortable place to sleep."

She couldn't argue with that. On Earth, he seemed to sleep easily even in the worst surroundings. Still, she hated to think of him caged down there while she got to enjoy a comfortable room.

"It is necessary to cage him," Egbor continued as if he were reading her mind. "An Argurma will only be under my control as long as I have complete control of you in his presence. Alas, I have to sleep, and cannot spend every moment threatening you. Even Azan, as fear-inspiring as she is, needs sleep on occasion. It is for everyone's safety that he is kept caged where he will not put everything at risk. Unlike Azan, when she came into my service, he has nothing else to lose but you."

From the corner of her eye, Terri noted the way the female's hand tightened around her fork, her expression hardening at Egbor's observation. The Blaithari second-in-command was not pleased by his comments. Whatever the history was between them, it lurked with a weighty presence behind those few words.

Terri directed her attention to her food. This was, without a doubt, the most uncomfortable meal she had ever shared with anyone—and given the way that she and Veral had shared a tense meal of lizards in the ruins of a building, that was saying something. Azan didn't speak, and Egbor watched her, a frown marring his brow as he seemed to realize that she wasn't going to perform for him.

Fuck that. She was here eating with him. She was doing only as much as she was required to.

He seemed to change tactics as he sat back and wiped his mouth, one hand gesturing to his surroundings.

"What do you think of my quarters, female?"

Setting her spoon down, Terri didn't miss the soft sigh from Azan but pretended not to hear it just as Egbor seemed to do after he cut his eyes in the other Blaithari's direction. Instead, she made a show of slowly looking around the room in admiration before finally allowing her eyes to meet his.

"It's nice," she said flatly.

His eyes blinked in surprise, and she was certain that she heard an amused snort come from the second-in-command.

"*Nice?*" he echoed. "All this splendor, the remainder of my fortunes as the younger son of a Blaithari prince and treasures accrued from plunder, and the best that you can come up with is… 'nice?'"

She swallowed the bite she had taken in the interim while he was busy boasting. A younger son of a prince turned to piracy… Interesting. He was watching her so expectantly for any reaction that—oh, what the hell—she would indulge him. Obviously, he was eager to impress upon her his importance. She couldn't imagine why. She was nobody, but if it would make the meal go faster, then she would bite.

"A prince, huh? Then why are you out pirating instead of enjoying a royal life?"

"It is a most incredible story," he said, the flinty look that had been in his eye since boarding eased as he settled back in his chair.

He drew a small tube out of his vest and followed by removing a pouch. Dipping his fingers into it, he withdrew a stringy mass that smelled sharply of the spicy fragrance floating around the room and stuffed it into the tube. Leaning back, he lit a small triangular nub at the end and took a deep drag on it. As the smoke billowed out from his lips, his pink scales flushed almost red, he almost made her think of a smoking dragon from one of the tattered children's book she had come across once in her youth.

"He publicly disgraced himself," Azan said, her tone somewhat bored as if she had heard this story too often. "He was exiled from his homeworld and all of the Blaithari colonies with nothing but this ship and a small crew to pilot it."

Egbor shot a dark look to the female, but he didn't snap at her like Terri thought he would. He seemed more inclined to continue to smoke whatever was in the hollow tube than exert any effort into retaliating. He pointed one thick finger at her and sneered.

"Be grateful that I find you too useful and amusing to terminate," he grumbled.

Azan grinned lazily at him, the first smile that Terri had seen on the female's face, and it was almost transformative. Transformative in that it made her seem even scarier than she appeared at rest. The hard, lethal edge to her smile was disconcerting. That the captain met her gaze with a nonplussed expression confirmed that this was a regular part of their odd relationship.

"You do not *attempt* to terminate me because we both know just how hard I am to kill. I make a better ally than an enemy, as you once pointed out."

He grunted in agreement and lifted a cup of some sort of dark, frothy substance to his mouth. Tipping back his cup, he drank long from it before setting it down with a hard tap on the table.

"Are you finished with your interruptions?"

"For now," Azan agreed.

He snorted and turned his attention back to Terri. "As Azan said, I was exiled in disgrace. It was considered an embarrassment to my family and peers that I sought profit in a rather lucrative natural resource on my planet, one that we have an abundance of."

Silence followed as he waited for Terri to play along.

"And what is that?" she asked.

Instead of answering directly, his expression turned smug and calculating. "Would you agree that there can be problems that arise when the population skews out of balance? When there is too much surplus of one that causes strain?"

"I can see how that could be possible," Terri replied slowly. She had seen just how crazy and covetous so many men became on Earth when women were harder for them to find, and the way women were shared among them in some sort of weird desperation.

"My homeworld, Blaitharsha, has a population ratio of two to three females to every male. It put considerable social pressure on males to take in additional mates and provide for them. For some families, it worked out well, for others... not so much. Economic and personal strain that can occur among those not equipped for it. I decided to do our populace a favor. Unfortunately, my family did not think much of my endorsement and funding for relocating surplus females of the lesser divisions of our society off planet."

Terri gaped at him. "You *sold* females to other species?"

"Ah, I see that you arrived at the same conclusion that my family did. Naturally there had to be some profit in the enterprise to keep it running. But each of them was sent to males who wanted them. When it came to light, I was stripped of all titles and permitted to take only my personal wealth, a small personal ship, and my flagship to live out the rest of my life comfortably in exile in space. Naturally, I did not leave without taking a little company," he grinned at Azan, who stiffened, her lip curling in a silent snarl. "But I was otherwise set adrift into the cosmos to wander aimlessly."

He took another drink and sighed in pleasure. "Unfortunately, having a loyal crew and a personal captive can only be amusing for so long. It is boring in space, and funds run dry if you like... indulgences," he said with a smirk as he puffed on the tube again. "Needless to say, despite my shrinking funds, it did not take me long to discover that all these trappings that were provided for me could be useful."

"You used it to attack ships, the way you got ours," Terri filled in. "You've been playacting the stranded royal for a long time, haven't you?"

"That I have, a role I play very well. But make no mistake, regardless of my noble birth, it does not make me a harmless male. Azan made that mistake, and I slit her throat and let her nearly bleed out until I had medical bring her back from the brink of death. I did this again and again until not even our medics could repair the flesh and her ruined voice, nor the scars that litter her body. I have claimed and branded every inch of her as my own. She thought she could get away from me and misjudged my strength and ruthlessness. Your mate, like so many other males, did likewise to their own peril. Now I possess you and your mate, and you are utterly mine until I decide to release you."

He chuckled unkindly as her food churned in her stomach. She felt sick.

"Do not waste your sympathy on Azan. I molded her into a ruthless and cruel killer, surpassing even myself, I do think. And once that happened, this female from common stock I gave the most vaulted position in my crew. She is merciless, my Azan."

He cast her a fond look, and the female Blaithari glared at him but didn't deny him as he reached and ran his hand over her breast affectionately before drawing away.

Egbor's humor faded as he recalled the food that wasn't being eaten. Tucking his tube back into his vest, he gestured impatiently.

"Let us eat and speak of more entertaining things—like what we can expect when we get to the planet."

"Jungles, vast rivers... and likely wildlife and predators lurking within both," Terri muttered as she turned her attention back to the cooling food in front of her. She wanted to reject the food. To say that it wasn't worth another minute in his company. She had gone days without eating before. The only thing that stopped her was the tiny life growing within her.

Hissing silently to herself, she grabbed a chunk of bread, slathered it with meat dripping with a gravy before taking a huge bite of it. It was delicious, savory, and juicy, but some part of her still had to choke it down as she forced herself to take another bite and another.

All she could think of was getting the meal over with so that she could get away from the disgusting Blaithari captain.

8

Veral glared at the bars of his cell. The meats, breads and savory foods did not tempt him. The small platter sat abandoned on the ledge that survived as a table to his left. Instead, he was watching the nervous movements of the small Blaithari male who had brought him his food. The youngling swiped the back of his sleeve nervously over his nose, his body trembling as he was pinned in place with fear.

Narrowing his eyes, Veral remembered that his mate had once said that he was terrifying without even trying. He did not wish to frighten the youngling. He wanted information. More than anything, however, he wanted to choke the life out of whatever male had allowed his offspring to live in such a deplorable state, scrawny—near starvation—with oversized worn clothes. At least he was not dirty, which, given the state of the lower levels of the pirate ship, was something of a miracle.

He must belong to someone higher up in the crew. Though the youngling was noticeably only half-Blaithari, he clearly belonged to someone with the means for basic, if inadequate, upkeep. He did not want to know what would happen to a youngling born in the lower levels of the pirate vessel. Some of the crew might have found an opportunity to eat him before he was even weaned. The thought of the male being raised in such an environment sickened him.

Cocking his head, Veral attempted to school his features into what he thought might be a sympathetic expression. The male backed away, his eyes widening in terror.

That did not work.

Veral hissed a curse beneath his breath, his mandibles clicking in agitation—which naturally did nothing to comfort the youngling. He then cursed whatever male sent him low into the ship to deliver him food. The small male was of an age where he should still be with his mother.

"Do not fear," he grumbled. "No harm will come to you from me. What is your name, and why are you not with your mother?"

The youngling hesitated and slid a cautious step forward. "Garswal. Mother died last year. One of the Igwin caught her when she was working."

"Your sire cares for you?"

He nodded. "He killed the Igwin and took me to the upper decks with him. I still have to do my job very well, but he makes sure I have some food and a warm place to sleep on the floor at the foot of his bed."

Growling, Veral turned away so he did not frighten the young male again. He had heard before how Blaithari males treated offspring born outside of a mating union, worse younglings born of mixed heritage. They were not considered Blaithari or legitimate offspring. This male was acknowledged only because his mother died, and his father took him in as one might a pet.

Stripping a large hunk of meat from his platter, Veral turned and held the offering out through the bars. The youngling's eyes widened, and he took another few steps forward before reining himself in reluctantly.

"I am not supposed to take anything without my father's

approval," he mumbled miserably, his eyes latched forlornly on the food held out to him.

Veral admired the youngling's self-restraint, uncommon for his age.

"That might normally be a sensible instruction, but there is no reason to not accept it from me. Argurma do not harm younglings, nor will I harm you. I am only disturbed by how small you are and wish to provide you with some sustenance that you so obviously require and desire."

Garswal swallowed, his expression filled with longing. "My father would not be happy with me taking some of your rations when I ate mine."

Veral's brow dipped in a heavy scowl, his vibrissae twitching around him in irritation. This did not make sense. "But you still hunger."

"He says that it is enough and as much as I have earned."

Clearly the youngling's sire was a male he would have to deal with personally once he escaped. A low growl rumbled from him, making Garswal twitch nervously. "Who is this male?"

"The… the captain. It is not so bad. His room is the best in the entire ship. It is more comfortable than what I had with mother, and I eat every day."

The cell filled with the deadly sound of vibrissae rattling and whipping as Veral's fury grew, instinctively searching for any weakness in the cell. That a male, especially one in a position to do much for his offspring, could treat his own youngling in such a way… With a deep breath, he clamped down hard on his anger, drawing it back under his iron control. He was frightening the small male. Still holding the meat out, he gave it a jiggle.

"Small males need far more to eat to grow healthy and strong. Eat. There is no surveillance in this room, and I will not speak of it to anyone."

Garswal crept closer, curious. "Is it true what they say about

Argurmas? Do you have tech implanted within you that makes you super strong and gives you the ability to be aware of active tech around you?"

"It is true." In part. "But it is very painful and begins when we are young. I would not recommend the process for other species."

The youngling let out a breath in fascination but nodded as he hastily reached forward and snatched the dangling meat from Veral's hand. He scurried back, no doubt driven by instinct as much as caution, before consuming the meat with his sharp teeth in several quick bites. The moment it was gone, he bobbed his head in thanks before darting out of the room before Veral could say anything more to him.

Drawing back into his cage, Veral settled on the sleeping pallet in the corner, his back sliding against the wall, the sharp horns on his shoulders scraping loudly against the metal. His vibrissae twitched from the sensation. He curled his lip as he took in his surroundings. The brig was rundown like most of the lower ship. It was clear that the captain was not invested in maintaining that part of the ship. It was disgusting.

Ignoring the food waiting for him, he closed his eyes and touched on that familiar pathway in his mind that connected him to his cousin. He knew that Kaylar would have been waiting for word since receiving the emergency alert. As expected, Kaylar connected with him immediately on their private communication frequency.

"Veral, where are you? The council is very displeased and have alerted the retrieval units. This is very serious, cousin."

The condemnation from Kaylar was so thick that he felt a wave of hostility curl through his systems from deep within him.

"Do you still have them fooled into thinking that you are not defective?" Veral shot back.

"And it shall remain so. You were unwise to mate and alert the council as to your emotional instability."

"I sincerely hope that you remember those words when you find a mate."

"It is fortunate that I am reasonable enough between the two of us that I will not risk such danger. Why are you transmitting to me? I estimated that it would be some revolutions before I heard anything of where you were hiding with your primitive mate."

"I was, but I require your assistance."

"This is ill timed, Veral. The council is very curious about the species you discovered a compatible mate in, as you likely are aware. I have been tasked with finding the location of the planet. The operatives who tracked the signal of your mate bonding disappeared, and with their disappearance, all record of where you were was lost."

"I am aware."

Silence greeted his statement as his cousin absorbed the meaning. A snort of disgust followed, proving that the male was in his typical foul temper.

"I assumed you were responsible for that. Must you do more to shame the clan? What exactly is it that you need?"

Veral snarled in frustration. He disliked admitting to his cousin that he had been captured, but it could not be avoided.

"My mate and I have been captured by pirates."

"Pirates…"

"Yes!" he growled.

"That is equally unfortunate and disgraceful. As I said, I have been tasked already with an assignment. I do not see how I will be available to help… unless…"

Veral gritted his teeth with a renewed aversion to the male firing through his processors. Terri was not going to be happy about this, but he would do whatever he had to in order to ensure the safety of his family. He had not even alerted other salvagers to the wreckage available on the planet as not to further disturb the species in whatever path they were bound to take, whether to extinction or evolution.

"I will give you the coordinates of Earth... the homeworld of the human species."

The silence fell heavily on the line, leaving nothing but empty static for such a long period of time that Veral wondered if he lost his cousin.

"Kaylar?"

"These terms are adequate. I accept. I will write the expenses off as part of the assigned mission. Send me your coordinates."

"I am transmitting to you now. We will be arriving on the planet in just a few days. I will attempt to slow the pirates down as much as possible until you arrive."

"Planet?"

"Yes. We were on assignment to salvage when we intercepted those that we assumed were stranded travelers."

"That was a grievous miscalculation on your part... What are the conditions?"

"Prepare to camouflage in dense foliage."

Kaylar hissed. *"Water?"*

"In plenty."

"You are attempting to jest..."

"Argurma do not possess much of a sense of humor that I am aware of."

"I hate you... Calculated route estimates my arrival in seven rotations. You are fortunate that I am close to that system."

"I thank you, cousin."

Kaylar growled but then let out a long sigh. *"Is it true that you bred with your mate?"*

"Terri carries my young," Veral confirmed.

"This is a blessing to our clan, no matter what anyone says. I will see you in seven days. Hold their position there. It would be

to our advantage to destroy our enemies from the ground rather than attempt to recover both of you from a ship."

"Agreed. I will be waiting."

Their connection went silent without another word exchanged between them. It was no different than other times he spoke to his cousin or any other member of his cursed family. His time with Terri had softened him that he felt affronted at all by the efficient termination. Shaking his head, he leaned forward and drew his food close to him. He was going to need his strength for what lay ahead of him.

9

Terri frowned at Azan as the Blaithari cleaned her claws with a short blade.

"Did anyone not tell you that staring is considered rude among many civilized species?" the female said, boredom heavy in her voice.

"And didn't anyone ever tell you that picking your nail... uh, claws—beside someone who's eating is disgusting?" Terri retorted over the bowl of some kind of stewed meat and bland white vegetables.

"You are awfully mouthy for someone I can snap in half with ease," the pirate pointed out. Her blade, in emphasis, lifted and pointed in Terri's direction as she spoke.

Terri set down her spoon and rolled her eyes. "Garswal, that would be—what?—the thirteenth time she's threatened me today."

"Fifteenth," the boy answered with a tiny, shy smile.

"Your point, little human beast?" Azan asked, her brow rising.

"Your behavior is predictable. You threaten me to get a reaction. It's childish. I've decided I'm not going to give you the satisfaction anymore."

"Is that so?"

The Blaithari female leaned forward and grinned, her yellow eyes gleaming.

"Yes," Terri replied flatly.

She didn't expect the pirate to lift a foot and kick out her chair from beneath her. It was just hard enough that the chair moved back several inches and jarred Terri. She fell forward with a startled gasp, her chest catching the bowl and splashing the contents everywhere. Stew dripping from her hair and down her nose, she looked up, leveling her nemesis with a hard glare. Bringing one hand up, Terri swiped the liquid from her face.

A low chuckle escaped Azan, surprising Terri. While often malicious or sneering, she had never heard a genuine laugh from the pirate before. The sound soon transformed to a fully belly laugh when Terri flung what was left in the bowl onto the female.

Wiping her own face, Azan grinned at her, her smile, for once, lacking bite. "You may be a soft, helpless little thing, but you have heart. I have to give you that. Not many would dare to throw their meal at me out of fear it would be their last. And in most cases, they would be right. But I like your spirit."

Terri raised an eyebrow, her expression guarded. "Thank you... I think."

Azan nodded as she stood and rooted around until she found some small cloths. She tossed one at Terri as she began to clean her face off. She shot Garswal an arch look. "I suspect that you found that entertaining."

The boy's laughter continued to bubble out of him freely as he nodded, his typically somber face—often far too serious for a boy so young—split with a wide grin. To her surprise, Azan didn't lash out at him. Instead, she ruffled his hair and smirked down at him.

"We will just keep this between us, though, yes? I do not want the other pirates to think I will not skin them alive if they try to disrespect me. This instance, I perhaps deserve. I just had to see if I could push the little human into reacting."

Azan's smile widened, her attention redirected at Terri as Garswal nodded in amusement and slipped out of her hold. She maneuvered around the table, her movements as silent and deadly as a predator.

"Watching you with the captain and the way you face every threat that constantly surrounds you here with barely a flinch confirmed that you are resilient, not easy to crush. True, you have the Argurma guaranteeing much of your safety, but he is not here to protect you from the little things that could easily happen. I notice all of this. At first, I thought that it might be a fluke, but you never fail. Seeing you stick up for yourself, I have decided that I like you, human. If you are an example of humanity, so strong despite being so fragile, it is a credit to your species. Do not mistake me. If it comes right down to it and I had to choose between the two of us, I would kill you if I must… but I would actually feel regret for it afterward."

Terri's brow furrowed. The pirate liked her. "I'm afraid I'm going to need a little more assurance than that. Where exactly does that put us now?"

The pirate shrugged, her expression relaxed and almost bordering on friendly. "It means a truce. I am still an opinionated, crude pirate who would sooner shoot someone than make pleasantries with them. But I will have your back in truth and do my best to make sure that you get out of this alive if I can, and not just as far as it serves that pompous ass Egbor's interests."

Terri nodded. "That sounds pretty fair. And what do you want in return?"

Yellow eyes widened at her in mock surprise. "I am not sure what you mean. Is my admiration and general amusement at watching Egbor fail to impress you or bring you under his thumb not enough?"

"Not really," Terri replied, a smile twitching at the corner of her own lips.

"Smart female. Another reason I can tolerate you breathing the same air in this room with me. You are correct. There is something more…"

"And what would that be?"

Azan leaned forward, her eyes cutting to Garswal, who had occupied himself with Azan's broken datapad. His rail thin body hardly seemed to take up any room on the bed as he hunched over it, his small, blunt claws tapping on the screen. Her voice lowered to a hiss.

"I want Egbor dead. Call it intuition, but I think your mate is going to be the only one who has a chance of accomplishing it, and that you have the strength to see this all to the end. That you will make certain that your male destroys him rather than letting him flee this planet. One way or the other, I do not want the captain leaving the planet's surface with the treasure of the *Evandra*," she whispered, her breath brushing Terri's ear in a lethal hiss.

At Terri's wide-eyed stare, the female rocked back on her heels, her voice returning to its normal volume as she brushed her hair over her shoulder with one of her hands. "Like I said, a truce. We throw our fates together on the planet."

"But you'll still kill me if you're ordered to—if you can't see a way around it?"

The pirate shrugged. "It would not be personal. But I have a feeling that the captain will know it is in his best interests not to give any such order, so that chance is small."

"I'm guessing this is the best offer I'm going to get, isn't it?"

"The best I can offer, I am afraid. No one on the ship will offer you better, that is for certain. I certainly wouldn't trust any of the males on this ship."

"But I can trust you?" Terri murmured doubtfully.

"Not really, but I will vouch for myself that I am the better bet."

Azan's expression continued to remain open and almost friendly in the face of Terri's concerns. In the end, the female was honestly giving Terri all the information she wanted to make an informed decision—and it was obviously in her favor to accept. In any case, despite the pirate being...well, a pirate, she hadn't been all that bad. Just annoying, more often than not, and occasionally amusing. More than anything, though, she had kept anyone from approaching and potentially harassing her. Hard as nails, she would make a good ally on the planet when she no longer had the buffer of private quarters.

"Very well," Terri said.

Azan's lips curled in a wicked grin as she threw an arm around her. "Good decision. You, me, and Garswal here are an excellent team. We will watch each other's backs on that death pit of a planet we are headed to."

The male glanced up, delight lighting up his face to be included as he eagerly nodded. Terri's stomach sank at the idea of the boy being at risk on a dangerous planet, but she knew that in the end neither she nor Azan would have any choice. Garswal was everywhere the captain was unless the captain wanted some time alone, in which case he was sent to their quarters. He would be going down to the planet, and no objection was going to change that.

She prayed that this alliance with Azan might spare all of them.

10

The air was wet. That was Terri's first thought as she exited the ship several days later when they finally arrived at their destination.

At first, she had been glad that they had finally arrived. Her mind had been filled with the anticipation of seeing her mate and some relief from being cooped up in her room with Azan for days. Even having Egbor hovering threateningly at her side as Veral was brought into the cargo bay had done little to dim her pleasure at being reunited with her mate.

She had wanted to run to his side, yet they were kept forced apart by Egbor's private guard and Azan as Veral was forced to fly a team of twenty pirates down to the planet surface to the nearest safe clearing. Still, she had been able to tell just from the way his eyes roamed eagerly over her that he had missed her just as much.

Theirs wasn't the only reunion denied that pained her.

The entire flight down, Krono could be heard throughout the ship snarling and digging at the metal door of the captain's quarters where he had been trapped. She was unsure how long he had been sedated, but she hoped that it was for a few days. She didn't want to think about him trapped and hungry in there, fed scraps of gods know what during the voyage. The captain hadn't wanted such a valuable animal dying before he could turn a profit from it. She hated hearing his cries and sounds of rage, being helpless to free him. It was almost a relief to leave the ship she had called home as she exited onto the planet surface.

Now, however, her first experience of the planet was a hell unlike anything she had imagined. Why was there water in the air? Her lungs burned as she labored to breathe. All her life, she had wondered what it would be like to live away from the desert and be somewhere lush and green, but nothing prepared her for the heavy drag on her lungs with every forced breath. She gasped and wheezed beneath her mate's concerned gaze. She could tell that he wasn't breathing comfortably either, but he seemed to be controlling his reaction better.

"What is wrong with her?" Azan demanded, her blaster leveling on Veral.

"She has never breathed such humid air before," he hissed impatiently. "She is a native of a desert environment like my species, and you thrust her out here without anything to make her manner of breathing easier. The humidity levels here are excessively high, even compared to the most humid places on her planet."

Egbor grimaced from where he stood off to the side, scouting the area as his chosen team from among the crew formed a perimeter around them. "I do not have anything like that, unfortunately. She will survive," he assured Azan. "You can see that, despite looking grotesquely wet and red, she is getting enough oxygen."

The Blaithari female did not look convinced, but Terri nodded. Breathing was uncomfortable, and the wetness in the air felt like it forced her to draw deeper breaths instinctively, but she was not suffocating from it.

Why had she ever thought that this would be a paradise?

The greenery was beautiful, especially laden as it was with strange, exotic flowers she could never have imagined. The centers of the flowers were brilliant pinks and reds and pushed out in frills and spirals and strange shapes that were hard to look away from.

Yes, despite everything, it was most definitely beautiful. She had to admit that.

It was just incredibly miserable, too.

Not only in terms of breathing comfortably, but her sweat beaded on her skin and dripped from her. She was hot, sticky, and sweaty. There was little doubt in her mind that if her suit wasn't self-cleaning and helping to regulate her body temperature she would have felt even worse.

Not that it helped with her general comfort level exposed to the elements. She hoped she got used to the humidity soon. She cast an envious look at the scaled assholes who didn't seem to have much external reaction to the conditions. The Blaithari and Turogo looked almost comfortable. Only the Igwin seemed to struggle a little, but even they didn't seem quite as uncomfortable as she was.

With a flick of his blaster, Egbor met Veral's eyes. "Lead the way, Argurma."

Veral snarled but looked away, his eyes searching out hers. As their gazes met, something within him relaxed as Terri gave him a reassuring nod, confirming that she was, in fact, okay.

His lips peeling back from his teeth, Veral gave the captain one more lethal glance that promised all manner of death and pain, before turning away to stride forward into the dense forest. Egbor stared after him with a self-satisfied smile as he shoved his pack into Garswal's arms at his side—his son, Terri had learned from Azan. Her disgust at the way the male treated his own offspring had clearly bothered her enough to satisfy Terri's curiosity about the relationship between the males.

The boy was always at the captain's side, tending to everything the older male wanted. She just hadn't expected him to be a son.

Who treated their own child that way?

Garswal struggled under the weight of the pack before he managed to get it looped securely around his body. Steadying himself, he looked up for approval just as the captain walked away, barking orders to the rest of the crew.

"Come on, ozu," Azan muttered to the child, nudging him forward. "The captain will be displeased if we fall behind. Are you going to be able to manage that?"

The look of disappointment fled from Garswal's features as he beamed up at her. "Yes, Azan, I will do good. I will keep up."

"Good," she muttered before tugging Terri along less than gently.

Even though Azan occasionally showed softer moments, she didn't let anyone forget that she was a ruthless pirate.

The spongy ground beneath their feet made walking a bit more awkward, and it had too much give to it for Terri's comfort. A thin layer of water seemed to cover everything. The rough, craggy trunks of the enormous trees surrounded them on all sides. She attempted to place her feet on their protruding roots when she caught sight of them, but they were sometimes spaced out too far apart. When there weren't roots nearby, she aimed for fluffy, dry patches of grass that occasionally rose above the water. The pirates picked their way with slow uncertainty ahead of her. That made Terri feel a little better, affirming that she wasn't the only one worrying about sinking into the wet muck.

"I had not anticipated this from the scans. The forest floor is similar to a bog. Step only where it is dry, or if you see green grass or flowers growing from the water. Anywhere dark or sandy, do not walk," Veral called back to her.

Swallowing nervously, she hopped over to a patch covered with tiny, delicate pink flowers just as a panicked screech rang out. Terri paused and glanced back, her mouth parting with horror.

An Igwin stood in the middle of a large section of ground that Veral had cautioned them about. Or at least he *had been* standing. Within the seconds between his bellow and Terri turning to glance back at him, he had sunk to his waist. His panicked shrieks and howls filled the air as his claws dug at the wet ground churning around him. He struggled to break free, but with every attempt, he sank deeper, faster.

Nausea swelled up into her throat, and Azan nudged her until she was forced to turn away. Garswal was safely tucked in between them, unable to catch sight of what was happening no matter how much he turned his head. It was just as well.

"You do not wish to see this," the second-in-command whispered.

Terri nodded. She most definitely didn't want to see it. His screams grew louder, but she tried to shut them out, her heart hammering. His death was going to be terrible.

She didn't take more than a handful of steps when the ground shook, and a deep hiss filled her ears. Jerking back around, a scream lodged in her throat. From a couple of floating masses of some sort of mossy substance, a giant serpentine head with a long, narrow snout rose from the murky water. Murky yellow-green eyes fixed on its prey.

The Igwin's limbs worked frantically, only his arms and head still free of the bog. He wailed again as the serpent's head lifted higher, its mouth gaping wide as an impossibly long tongue flicked out, tasting the air. In the blink of an eye, its head whipped down. Long jaws closed around the male, and he let out more pitiful scream as it yanked him out of the mud and pulled him back down into the water between the floating masses of plant material.

Silence fell among them, and everyone seemed frozen in shock until two more serpents pushed up from the water.

"Run!" Veral roared.

In a panic, everyone surged forward. Everyone except Veral. Though he was a short distance ahead, he was barreling back toward them, his eyes pinned frantically on her. He didn't stop until the captain stumbled to a halt, raised his blaster, and pointed it at her. Egbor's breath wheezed out him fearfully, but his hand did not shake as he kept the weapon leveled in her direction.

"Lead the way to safety," the captain snarled. "If you do not save us, you will not be saving her either."

The sound of rushing water and scraping was getting louder. Terri didn't have to look behind her to know the creatures were heading in their direction. Azan's arm suddenly banded around her, lifting her up over the larger female's shoulder. Terri swayed as the Blaithari stooped to snatch up Garswal in her other arm.

"Hurry!" she shouted as she began to hop from one patch of ground to the other, hauling both charges over the terrain as fast as possible.

Veral let out a roar of frustration, his mandibles stretching wide and his vibrissae, which seemed to be in moving in a highly agitated state since they stepped out onto the planet, whipped faster. Craning her head around, she watched as his eyes narrowed on Azan before he spun around and sprung forward.

Terri didn't know what unspoken message passed between them, or what he saw in the Blaithari female in that moment, but whatever it was, he had decided to trust the female to get Terri away.

Flopped helplessly over Azan's shoulder, Terri dropped her head. Her neck ached from the angle at which she had held it. It had the unfortunate side effect of providing her with an unhampered view of the creatures hunting them.

Their long bodies seemed slowed down a little as they whipped themselves in a rapid glide over the top of the mossy surface. Their mouths, full of sharp teeth, opened wide. Webbing fanned from both sides of their head in intricate, boney fins as they neared, preparing to strike. Terri did scream that time when one shot forward to snatch a Blaithari, a male she didn't recognize, off his feet. His scream joined hers, but was cut off as the serpent slipped back into the water.

Her scream didn't have time to quiet when the second serpent snapped up a squealing Turogo, ripping him away from his companions. They tried to fight the creature for him, each with one of their hands gripping him tightly while the other hand fired their blaster upon the monster until the very last moment when the creature yanked him away, breaking their grasp on him. The serpent didn't waste time. Its body careened back, splashing into the water, the male's shocked gaze burning into Terri's mind as he disappeared with it, his torso caught in its mouth.

The other males of his group did not even try to catch up after that. Even as they shrank in the distance, Terri watched as the three other males of his group dropped to the ground in grief. The anguished cries of the males continued long after he vanished into the water. They were nearly out of sight when they cried out again as the ground of the floating plant matter near them pushed up and away once more, and she was able to make out more serpents rising to put the grieving males out of their misery.

She didn't even realize she was crying until Azan's voice met her ear.

"Save your grief. The Turogos are spawned in symbiotic packs. They would not have lasted long without their brother. They waited for their souls to be carried to rejoin him. This is their way," Azan whispered fiercely. "If you must, direct your emotion to the male who leads them and let it burn. Many will die in this place, between the creatures of this world and your mate's vengeance. I am certain of it. But not me."

The assurance in the female's voice reminded Terri of just how much of a survivor Azan was. Everything could burn down around her, and regardless of what she might feel for the plight of the others, she wouldn't allow herself to go down with it. Terri understood. She had been there herself. If not for Veral, she would still be looking out only for herself. But she had more to worry about now.

They had to survive. There was no other option.

At least there were no further sounds of pursuit. Whatever those snake creatures were, they had given up the chase to consume their prey. It made her ill to consider that it could have been any of them who ended up in the bellies of the creatures. It sickened her further that her belly growled now, of all times.

To her surprise, Azan's body shook with her quiet chuckle.

Of course that would amuse the pirate.

Eventually, Azan came to a stop, depositing Terri and Garswal on the small stretch of firm ground that the crew was clustered nervously upon. Terri wanted nothing more than to push her way through everyone and find Veral, but the warning look in Azan's eyes kept her in place. The female was drawing deep, ragged breaths and shook her head. Terri understood why as she turned and met the cold gaze of the captain fixed on her.

Egbor was always watching and could retaliate on anyone for the smallest infraction to his rules.

Giving the captain her back, she settled for peering among the crew, searching for a glimpse of her mate's dark head. A gasp of relief left her lips when she caught sight of him. Just beyond the milling bodies, Veral, standing nearly a head taller than everyone else, was also scanning the small crowd, scowling until he caught sight of her. His glowing blue eyes flared, and he pushed through the bodies separating them, his gaze moving over her anxiously.

Once assured that she wasn't injured, he calmed as he stood the few feet that he was allowed near her. His fingers stretched out before fisting tightly at his side, his mandibles clicking at a distressed tempo. His eyes cut to the captain, who tapped his blaster meaningfully. Veral growled but turned his attention back to Terri, his gaze piercing her with such intensity that she knew without a doubt that he would slaughter every one of them if he had any assurance that he would be able to escape with her.

Somehow, their restrained proximity to each other created an invisible barrier between them that everyone seemed to feel and acknowledge. The crew gave them their berth. Everyone except an upper crew Blaithari, who attempted to shove him out of the way with the intent to approach the captain, but he was unsuccessful. Veral's arme snapped out and with one fast move pushed the male into the loose sediment of the bog. The Blaithari's bellow had everyone on dry land scrambling to pull him out, but Veral barely shifted an inch the entire time that the crew hastened to save their own, his eyes fixed on her as if he couldn't bear to move them away for even a moment.

"Looks like everyone is here. We will keep moving until sundown," Egbor called out, his flinty stare sweeping over his crew. Wisely, no one protested. "Mind where you step so that you do not end up like the fools who were eaten, and stay away from the Argurma unless you want to take an unexpected bath."

Several weary chuckles rose in response to the captain's remark as eyes turned on the soggy Blaithari male. He snarled at them all before directing a look full of hate at Veral. Her mate, as usual, did not appear concerned with the threat issued. Just the opposite. His lips curled in a chilling smile of anticipation. Casting one more glance full of promise to Terri, Veral strode over and leaped to the next dry mass.

A small group of Turogos watched him with blank stares but nodded their wide heads in a sort of silent agreement among themselves as they proceeded to navigate together over the ground a short distance away. They kept close, moving as a team in a practiced manner that suggested that they were perhaps more familiar with this sort of environment than any of them.

As they followed after Veral, the rest of the crew trickled forward. The captain was surrounded the entire time by his personal guards and no others, though the crew moved like a wall as they crossed the bog nearby. Terri felt a small hand slip into hers as she stared after them. Startled, she looked down and met the concerned gaze of Garswal. She squeezed his hand reassuringly as Azan stepped up to his opposite side. The female handed both of them a hydration pod. Terri gratefully placed it in her mouth and bit down it. Bursting with a small pop, it immediately dissolved, leaking cool liquid down her throat.

"Stick close by my side," Azan said quietly. "I don't trust any of this."

Terri nodded, her jaw tightening, as they kept pace with the crew. Nothing about this place could be trusted. Ultimately, she knew that included Azan as well.

11

High in the branches, Veral watched the crew slump with exhaustion in whatever small hollow or groove they could find among the tight network of roots. Though they stumbled around, half-blind, led by the handheld lights they carried, Veral's vision was unhampered, eyes glowing with perfect night vision. From his vantage point, he knew that the roots were perhaps the safest place to rest that they could hope for without constructing a shelter.

The massive trees grew so close together that their long branches would block out most of any rain that might fall overnight. The roots themselves offered further shelter. At some point, they had forced each other up from where they were anchored in wet earth, creating natural beds amid the dips and hollows they formed above the wet ground. Everyone was all the more eager to seek shelter among the roots as they scoured the area for any sign of predators.

His eyes slid over them all, coming to rest on the form of his mate as she stretched out the kinks in her back. She tilted her head back as if sensing him lurking above her, smiling as she met his gaze. Discreetly, she pressed her fingers to her lips—blowing him a kiss, she called it.

The corners of his mouth quirked in response, his heart warming at the gesture. He touched his own lips, fingertips sliding between the gap between his mandibles in silent communication of his returned love. Her smile widened, but then she ducked her head, her attention turning abruptly to the female at her side.

He understood why, but he ached with disappointment. It was ironic for a male who spent so long ignoring every emotion that reminded him of how flawed he was in the eyes of his species. Yet now he acknowledged the need that boiled inside of him to be joined with her again.

Skimming over the other males, his eyes fell at last on the source of his current problems. Egbor strutted below with his personal guards as he sought the best sleeping accommodations. Coming across a spot that he wanted, he ousted the male who was already occupying it in order to make his own bed on the green plant life that covered the expanse of the bog lodged between two curved roots. Even as he lay there among them, the ridiculously expensive weave and stitching on his robes made him stand out among his crew. He looked like a pampered idiot. It was a deceptive and cultivated appearance.

And at that moment, there was no one that Veral hated more.

This planet should have been a private place where he could leisurely explore with his mate while they worked side by side. Instead, he was forced to see her under constant threat. He did not doubt that the second-in-command—Azan, she was called—would do all that she could to keep Terri from harm. Whenever she stood near his mate, her bearing had an attentive protectiveness to it, daring anyone to approach.

But he also knew that the female had iron in her that had been fashioned and tempered by the fires of pain and cruelty. He could see it within the depths of her eyes, cold and merciless.

Right now, she was biding her time, waiting for some sign of the advantage she sought. He knew that she wanted to kill the captain. It burned within her eyes whenever she watched Egbor unnoticed. She hated the male even more than Veral did, of that he had no doubt. But to preserve her life and position, much the same thing for a female in a pirate crew, she would kill his mate if ordered. If that happened, then Veral would be forced to slaughter her along with everyone else.

Although sometimes it was easy to forget when he was with his mate, he too was a cold, merciless killer, after all.

Movement in the distance attracted his attention, and he stilled. One of the Blaithari males was moving away from the safety of the trees. Veral's eyes tracked him, following the male's unsteady movement over the solid mounds in the bog, his hands trailing along the sides of trees to stabilize himself whenever he came within reach of one.

Veral leaped down from the tree, taking to the shadows. Most of the pirates had already drifted off to sleep. The few males who had been left on the first shift of guard duty were easy enough to avoid as he silently stalked after his prey.

Drawing nearer, a hard smile pulled at his lips. It was the Blaithari who had attempted to shove his way between Veral and his mate. Right now, however, he was looking around furtively while he made his silent escape.

Where was he sneaking off to?

The male still smelled of the bog water and bits of sediment that clung to him. At some distance from the camp, he stopped and ducked behind a tree. Veral climbed into the tree to give him a better vantage point as he watched his target dig into his bag and pull out a long narrow pipe and a folded white cloth. Sitting down at the base of the tree, the male set the cloth on his thigh and unfolded it review a pinch of tangwal gum.

Veral tilted his head. Tangwal gum was an expensive—and highly addictive—drug and aphrodisiac. It was known to be difficult to obtain except by those who knew the right contacts. It explained why the male had crept away under darkness. The smoke had a distinctive spicy scent and, if one didn't smoke it regularly and build up a resistance to its side effects, would stimulate an intense sexual arousal.

A plume of smoke rose in the air, and Veral wrinkled his nose at the overbearing stench. This was the perfect opportunity to catch the Blaithari unaware. His muscles tightened, preparing to drop on the male...

"Status report," Kaylar broke through, interrupting Veral as their private frequency opened in his mind.

Catching himself, he snarled silently as the branch beneath him creaked, making his target jump to his feet and scurry away from the tree. The male's uncertain eyes flicked around; his pipe clenched firmly in his mouth. Veral stilled among the foliage, glad for its thickness that obscured him as he watched and waited for the male to let down his guard again.

"Stable. We arrived planetside. As expected, the captain, lacking a suitable ship to land in these conditions, had me pilot my own ship down to transport his crew."

"That is fortuitous. It will make the situation easier. Disable transmissions between the landing team and the pirate vessel, kill the pirates, disable pirate ship, escape. This will be so easy it will be like a vacation. What is your plan?"

"We are taking the scenic route."

"Repeat?"

Veral chuffed to himself. He had already began integrating some of his mate's more peculiar and colorful phrases.

"Something my mate says that refers to intentionally taking a longer route."

"That is nonsensical. What does the view have to do with plotting a route?"

"I believe it originally refers to taking routes designed for pleasure rather than expediency."

"Your humans are an absurd species," Kaylar scoffed.

Veral could not argue that absurdity was a big part of human culture from what he had gleaned.

"Regardless, going the longer route over the region's hazardous terrain has been successful in delaying the pirates."

"Casualties?"

"Only the four males who fed the local wildlife."

"I am beginning to question whether or not we had the same warrior training, cousin."

Veral bared his teeth at the open mockery in his cousin's transmission. His vibrissae whipping around him, he moved through the branches, sliding back toward the opening above the Blaithari who had settled once more against the tree. The pungent smell of the tangwal gum still hung in the air, but it was joined by the overpowering scent of male musk that offended his scent receptors. Glaring down in disgust, he curled his lip at the pirate eagerly stroking himself.

The male began to grunt, his thighs quivering, and Veral's muscles coiled, his vibrissae sliding through the air as they vibrated. The mate at least had the opportunity to enjoy one last pleasure, though Veral saw more than he ever wanted to of a Blaithari's genitals.

Dropping down to the pirate's side, Veral landed in a crouch and slammed back the thick horn jutting out from just above his elbow into his target's neck. Thick streams of ejaculation splattered on the twitching thighs just barely within Veral's line of vision. Though the sounds of the nearby nocturnal creatures went silent, the wet, gurgling sound that followed was quiet as the pirate choked on his own blood as he exsanguinated.

Veral yanked his arm forward as he stood, the slurp of the flesh detaching from the horn preceding the soft thump of the body as it fell to the ground. Turning, he glanced at it dispassionately before propping one foot on the side of the corpse and kicking it into the dark, wet soil. He lingered at the edge of the treacherous earth only long enough to watch as the remains slowly sank. Only when it was completely obscured from sight did he turn away to begin his trek back to camp.

"Five down," he growled to Kaylar.

"Be certain to practice some restraint and not kill them all before I arrive," his cousin said.

With a snort, Veral rinsed the blood from his body in a pool of water, his internal scans searching for any sign of approaching lifeforms. That accomplished, he turned away and left the pipe and cloth abandoned at the base of the tree among the splatters of blood.

The evidence remaining would be enough to convince Egbor that the male had been killed by something in the forest while he was attempting to enjoy what he had pilfered from the captain's cabin.

It did not take him long to return to camp. Though the guards had shifted positions to spread out further, eyes fixed on darkness of the surrounding forest, no one had noticed his absence nor marked his return.

Veral slipped easily back into the tree, resuming his place over where Terri slept. As he crouched once more upon the limb, he saw Azan's eyes open as she met his gaze. She gave nothing away of her thoughts, nor did she make any attempt to alert anyone. She inclined her head to him before rolling on her side and dismissing him.

He frowned at her back until his attention was pulled once

more to his mate. Terri's face was relaxed in slumber, so he was startled when her eyes opened. Relief spread across her face. She must have noted his absence and had been worrying while he was away. Although her human vision was terrible, he had no doubt that she was able to pinpoint his presence by the glow of his eyes.

Not wishing his mate to feel further distress, Veral crooned softly down at her as he stretched out on his belly on the branch to lie over her.

"Anastha, sleep," he whispered. "I am here."

"Veral," she sighed, her eyes drifting shut once more as she curled against the youngling burrowed between her and Azan.

Lifting his head, his eyes narrowed on an animal slinking through the branches, enormous wings angled at its side. It must have flown into the tree while he was away. Its head dropped down, wings unfurling as it prepared to fall upon the females, likely targeting the youngling between them.

Hissing, Veral snapped to his feet and yanked it from the branch. It snarled, twisting in his arms and attempting to dig its claws into the tough material of his armor. Veral gripped the underside of the creature's jaw and snapped it viciously. When the animal dropped to hang limply in his grasp, he threw it a short distance from the tree, where it would doubtlessly be discovered. He stared down at its corpse, his mandibles clicking as he wrestled his aggression back under control before returning to his place on the branch.

Dropping once more above his mate, he lay there, watching over her, until sleep claimed him. They would both need their rest.

12

The missing male from the upper crew was on everyone's lips as they cast cautious glances around them. Even Egbor seemed to be more on edge, though he had publicly denounced the male as a traitorous creature who deserved to be eaten.

That was the official consensus after the team returned with the damning evidence of all that remained of the Blaithari. It had been little more than a scrap of fabric that reeked like the stuff that the captain enjoyed smoking and another long smoking tube. At the sight of them, the captain had flushed red and spat upon the ground with a string of curses. As far as he was concerned, it was clear that the male had stolen from him, and had snuck off to enjoy it when he was eaten for his trouble.

That was the accepted version of events, and it wasn't far from the truth—though Terri knew the true creature that killed him, and it was nothing that came from the forest. She had been afraid when Veral disappeared, worried that something terrible would happen to him. When he returned, she had been too relieved to care where he had been.

All that mattered was that he made it back safe.

She understood now exactly where he had been. He had stalked the male and killed him. Terri had no tears to shed over the pirate, but worry plagued her ever since the call of alarm had gone up that someone would suspect him.

To her surprise, no one voiced outright suspicion against Veral, though the pirates seemed to give him a wider berth. It hadn't escaped their attention that the male who had angered the Argurma was the one among their company who had ended up dead, even if his reason for leaving the safety of their numbers had been unrelated. The males whispered among themselves about the Argurma, spinning together what they knew of the species with wild speculations. Among the more farfetched of them was that Veral had the ability to enrage wild animals and summon them into attacking by the use of some implant or another.

No one, however, pinned it directly on him.

As far as anyone had seen, the Argurma never moved from his tree, not even when search parties scattered over the surrounding area. He watched everything from the branch where he reclined, unconcerned. In fact, a large predator with pale marbled skin and long leathery wings that lay dead nearby reinforced the perception that he worked hard to keep the crew safe—and in turn keeping his mate safe in the process. Therefore, by their reasoning, ill fortune would only fall upon any who directly offended the male.

Terri had no doubt that he heard everything because every now and then his lips curved in a slight show of humor. The expression was so small that she might have missed it if she weren't looking directly at him. If any of the pirates had happened to glance at him, they would have been greeted with the sight of a male disdainfully ignoring them, his eyes for no one but his mate.

As flattering as that was—and it warmed her heart to know that she was the most important thing on that planet to him—she wasn't stupid. His gaze tracked her, but she had no doubt that he was listening to the pirates and monitoring everything they did from his position. As of yet, no one had seemed inclined to leave the tight cluster of trees, and Egbor's attention was directed toward rallying the crew. A number of males were shouting to return to the ship and leave the cursed world and the tomb of the Evandra behind.

"That male is an idiot," Azan muttered from where she leaned against a nearby tree, her attention focused on the captain as he waved his blaster around. "They know he will not fire just yet. Unfortunately, he will kill someone as an example soon if they push him hard enough, despite the fact that he cannot afford to just throw away the males who do all of his dirty work for him. Not that he isn't working hard to get us all killed anyway, ever since he took the Argurma hostage. This venture is the errand of a fool," she muttered as she shoved away from the tree to join Terri by her side.

Terri's lips thinned as Egbor drew near his limit and fired into the air. The crew, who had been shouting over each other, fell into silence as the captain sneered. Though his other five hands were currently free of weapons, they hung tense at his sides in a show of aggression and dominance.

"Silence, all of you! I will hear no more superstitious blathering. Do I need to remind you of how much fortune awaits us once we find the *Evandra*? The entire crew will be wealthy beyond anything you could dream. Focus on that alone. It is worth every risk. We will drink, and feast and fuck! We will have every pleasure laid before us!"

The uncertain mumble shifted to interest as the captain continue to shout out promises of excesses, and more than one male nodded along eagerly.

Terri grimaced at the cheap trick. Sway the masses by telling them that they would be given the very things they desire. It was how the gang gained a foothold in Phoenix, so it wasn't something she had never seen before. Although a few males showed reluctance, the majority of the crew hastened to gather their supplies in preparation to depart.

"Veral," Egbor called out as he moved toward the base of the tree. Planting his lower hands on his hips, he glowered up, meeting the Argurma's cold eyes. Terri could practically feel the tension coiling in the air between them. The captain extended an empty hand out to the forest. "So far, despite our losses, you have done well guiding us. It is time. If you care about the safety of your female, we shall continue on."

Her mate didn't reply. His eyes shifted to her seconds before he dropped soundlessly from the tree. Even the impact of his feet hitting the ground was light as his crouched body connected with the turf, a hand slightly outstretched for balance. His claws were out, and they dragged against the ground as he drew back and slowly stood, his menacing glare fixed on the pirate captain.

For his part, Egbor didn't appear even remotely fazed. His expression was hard and emotionless as he lifted a second blaster from its holster and pointed it directly at her.

"Just so that we are very clear here on who holds all the power," he said with a chilly smile.

"For now," Veral agreed.

A burst of laughter escaped the pirate and he shook his head. "As amusing as this all is, there is something of a time schedule involved here—my own. There is only so long before someone notices my ship orbiting around the planet. I must insist that we continue. Now."

A rattling growl rose from Veral as he turned away and stalked by her, yet as he passed, she felt his vibrissae slide against her cheek and the glide of his hand against her own before he was gone. Terri stared after him, frustration brewing within her.

She hated being so helpless.

A weapon prodded her, and she turned to meet Egbor's

amused gaze. From the corner of her eye, she noted that Azan had stiffened at her side.

"Do not get any ideas, little female," he said. Then he dropped the blaster and holstered it. "Just a small reminder that your well-being is entirely in my hands. You would do well to cooperate and make certain that I continue to have a use for you."

"If anything happens to me, Veral will destroy all of you," Terri returned.

The captain inclined his head in agreement. "If I kill you, yes. But this is a dangerous place, and accidents do happen." His lips curved into a sharp smile before his eyes dropped on the boy at their side. "Come, Garswal, you will walk with me today. It appears we will be walking through a thicker stretch of forest. I suspect there will be some need to clear the route. Might as well have your blade at the ready."

With that reminder, he walked away, his guards joining him as they followed along the path that Veral was cutting through the forest, Garswal struggling to keep up at their heels.

Even from that distance, Terri could see the thick vines hanging low from the trees, obstructing the path. Several males were already hacking at them with blades, though Veral seemed to slip through them without trouble, his vibrissae moving around him as he found the easiest path. It seemed that the pirates were well underway. Only a few lingered to bring up the rear, their eyes resting on Azan and Terri.

"Move on," Azan hissed impatiently with a sharp nudge.

Terri stumbled forward but didn't take it personally. The female was still staring off into the distance, her eyes filled with concern as they followed Garswal's slow progress as he began to cut away the vines nearest to the captain.

"He will be okay, won't he? I mean, the captain wouldn't put his own child in danger..." Terri began, hoping to reassure the female.

Azan barked out a disdainful laugh as they pushed forward. "You haven't been around Blaithari long enough to understand. Garswal is useful to him. That he sired him merely makes him possessive of him as any other belonging, but not out of any paternal affections. My father was a loving male... He never would have put me in danger like that. But Garswal, he is only half-Blaithari... and among many males, particularly among the nobles, that makes him only half a person. Definitely not a son. His only purpose is to serve Egbor. The captain will kill any male who harms him but will use the youngling and sacrifice him without thinking twice about it."

Terri's teeth sank into her bottom lip as they stepped into the gradually thickening brush. She was startled at how quickly the terrain shifted as they began to climb from the spongy flatlands. The salvage was located among the ravines, from what she recalled of the schematic. This meant that they were leaving the boggy terrain for the dangerous cliffs of the inner forest.

She swallowed nervously as loose rocks and soils shifted out from under her feet. They were only beginning their ascent, but a cold sweat broke over her at the thought of falling from the side of the cliffs, the captain's words haunting her. With firmer ground and thicker cover, there was also a greater chance of dangerous predators concealed within the forest.

Terri shivered as tall plants grazed her in passing. Though she could only marginally feel them through the protective layers of her armor, every brush skittered over her nerves as if something far more dangerous were pacing beside her.

She desperately missed Krono. His presence would have helped settle her nerves at least a little in the unfamiliar environment. Higher they climbed at a ground-eating pace, one that left her wheezing and weak-legged by the time the sun began to drop in the horizon. She was all but ready to collapse when an excited shout rose from the crew.

Something had been discovered.

Squinting, Terri pushed through the remaining brush, her breath leaving her in a gasp. Just ahead, leaning at an awkward level, was a large structure. It was covered in vines and various plant life that sprung up where dirt had collected, but even she could see that it had once been part of a starship.

Egbor's voice rose over the crew, his shout triumphant. "We are on the right track! And tonight, we will rest securely in shelter."

13

Although a large hole had been ripped into the side of the wreckage, Veral was surprised at how well preserved the section of the ancient starship was. Indeed, aside from the hole itself, most of the wreckage was secure and easily contained the entire crew that were currently settling within it with plenty of space to spare.

That this torn-away section had survived near intact was marvel of engineering. Most ships that he was familiar with, if they were torn apart upon entry, would not have much remaining to be suitable for shelter. The Elshavan created technological marvels that he would have discounted as fantasy if he were not seeing it with his own eyes and scanning it with his own systems.

He was only somewhat familiar with the lore of the *Evandra*. Just the bits and pieces he had been able to find from the Yil'anip databases when he had been assigned the salvage. The House of Grez'na were an ancient line of the species and contained the best records that could be found regarding their oldest predecessors.

In their records had been details of an ancient star faring race, the Elshavan, who held great wealth and technology. The most prized of their ships was the *Evandra*, the vanquisher of foes. When the Elshavan went to war with another great power, the Diralthax, all the planets between their civilizations became the battlegrounds, and chief among their outposts had been the planet Yil'winar. Though the Elshavan won, the *Evandra* was lost to them, taking with it not only the prince and all his royal wealth that was traveling upon it, but also war tech that seemed more legend than truth.

Eventually both the Elshavan and Diralthax civilizations collapsed and became a curiosity of galactic scholars who were still uncertain just how much of the lore surrounding the civilizations was factual. Little remained of them outside of a few written accounts and the trace lore on planets that fell under the control of their civilizations. No one had even so much as located the homeworlds.

Naturally, when taking the assignment, Veral believed that the Elshavan had probably not been as advanced in tech as the then-primitive Yil'anip.

Now, as he looked at the perfectly seamless black walls that not even the Argurma with all their tech advances could accomplish, he was not so certain. In some places, he was sure that he could see faint lines of what might have been data outlays and storage compartments, but he could not discern any way to open the latter. The pirates were going to be disappointed if the ship itself, when they found it, was more of the same rather than brimming with wealth waiting to be claimed.

As it was, the males following him into the wreckage were grumbling at how empty everything was as they searched for any sign of wildlife that may have taken refuge within it. The absence of any trace remains of the normal things one might find in the wreckage of a manned ship disturbed them as much as the lack of any signs of animal habitation.

It was odd. His scans did not pick up any animal matter. The only organics he could detect were the bits of plant material that had managed to blow inside. Even more curious, there was an unidentifiable hum of energy coming from somewhere that he could not source. That alone pricked at his systems as he struggled to identify it. Even his vibrissae could not find any source for it in the electric currents running through the air.

"I am telling you, this place is haunted," a Blaithari male muttered to the male nodding at his side.

Interesting.

Terri had made an offhand comment about cursed gold once in jest. The Argurma had complicated belief systems regarding ancestors but did not believe that the dead remained in the living world.

Yet he could not dismiss the fact that there was something peculiar about the broken-away section of the Evandra. Not spirits of the dead... but something of the people remained. Something that deterred even wild animals from attempting to make it their home.

"There is nothing here," the other male whispered to his companion. "Not even a table or a handheld device. Nothing. It is unnerving. What if the rest of the ship's remains are just like this?"

"I do not like that we are risking our lives for possibly nothing," the first male returned with a vexed hiss.

"Do not be speaking ill of the *Evandra*," Egbor snapped as he came up behind them.

Veral cocked an ear in his direction, his systems always in some part locked on the captain, as the male continued to speak tersely.

"We have no understanding of how their tech worked, but I have no doubt that when wealth is spoken of, it is tangible, for the legends to speak so freely of it in our stories as much as in those of our Yil'anip neighbors. This is but a small, inconsequential part of the ship. It will serve our purpose well enough by doing nothing more than providing our shelter for the night."

"I still say it is haunted," muttered the first male the moment the captain moved away. "Even for an ancient, advanced race... this is unnatural."

Veral chuffed silently to himself in amusement. There was nothing supernatural about it, just currently unidentifiable. The whispers brought to mind all the ridiculous things the crew had been spouting about him earlier that same morning.

The unknown inspired fear. This was nothing new.

He did not fear it, but now he was deeply curious about the Evandra. If he could manage to retrieve anything at all before leaving the planet, it could be an opportunity to learn something about their technology. Possessing knowledge not held by his brethren could give him an edge when it came to avoiding them and keeping his mate safe.

Arriving at the end of the wreckage, he spied the area that was segmented off from the rest by two partial walls with an open passageway. There was an impression in the center of the room that appeared as if something was designed to lift up from the floor, and many more of the outlines of storage units on the walls.

This time, however, there was an obvious outline of what appeared to be a data unit fixed to the wall. He skimmed his fingers over it. At his touch, something foreign linked to his systems.

His natural instinct was to recoil at the touch of the unfamiliar tech, but was distracted when the screen suddenly blinked on, glowing faintly. He cocked his head and peered at it. It seemed to be a basic medical diagram, from what he could tell. Three images were side by side showing the species' skeletal, muscular, and vascular systems. Curious, he dropped his hand away and leaned forward, only to have the screen go dark.

Very interesting.

Veral touched it again, the tech once more flooding through his system as it uplinked. The path was strange. The moment he released contact, he was unable to maintain it. It unraveled rapidly. Like all channels, it would require considerable practice building a path with it. *If* he had the time. He would need to salvage something small, preferably from the primary wreckage, to explore it further.

Eyes leaving the screen, he focused again on the indention in the floor. He walked forward and tapped his foot on it.

Nothing.

Pacing around it, his eyes fell on a lighter plate on the dark material. He stepped there but this time did not lift his foot. The uplink, as before, was instantaneous. The flooring within the impression parted, and a large metal pad lifted up before fully extending into an obvious med-bed, the sensors along the side lighting up in anticipation of a patient. He stepped away, testing how long he could maintain the connection. It lasted for several minutes before everything flickered off. The table, lacking the necessary power and instructions to retract, remained in the center of the room.

He tapped a claw on his thigh as he regarded it. He considered attempting to retract it, but the sounds of the crew were getting closer. Moving away, he approached the panels and set his hand on them one by one. Not many opened. Some flashed a request for an access code. Those that did open had what seemed to be basic medical supplies.

It was not impressive, but perhaps to be expected. When it came to basic emergency supplies, little changed over time. Even Argurma warriors depended on bandages in the field before they could be treated by a medic.

The last cabinet slid shut, and he yanked his hand down just as the thudding of boots approached. Turning away from the wall, Veral faced the male who walked in, a look of interest on his face.

"Fascinating," Egbor murmured, his eyes coming to rest on the med-bed. "Have you discovered anything?"

Veral lifted his shoulders, mimicking his mate's shrug. "As you can see, that looks like a med-bed. It would appear that this was the ship's medical bay."

"Pretty sparse for medical," the captain observed.

"The med-bed appears standard, and the screen there would have received data," Veral replied, pointing to the data unit's screen. "There is a high probability that whatever had been in this room and this part of the ship fell out when it ripped away from the frame of the *Evandra*." There was a degree of truth to that statement.

The captain nodded. "So it would seem," he muttered to himself as he began to walk away. At the entrance, he paused and glanced over at Veral. "You would not attempt to deceive me, would you, Argurma?"

Veral only blinked at him. "To what purpose would that serve? My only interest is to keep my mate safe."

"And what of your duty to your employer?"

"There is no duty greater than her," Veral growled impatiently.

That was the complete truth. Whatever the prince had planned to pay him for the salvage was meaningless in the face of Terri's safety. He would abandon it without regret. The likelihood of anyone else being able to salvage it was small since few species had the ability to detect lifeforms to a degree that they would be able to avoid them. Though he jested with his cousin about taking a scenic route, he had made certain that nothing dangerous would get anywhere near his female. Other salvagers would need incredible luck to survive against the dangers of this forest.

Egbor nodded. "Some would say that is dishonorable, to set aside your contracts so easily, but I can respect it. The funny thing about you Argurma, with all your hard, cold logic, is that you are so incredibly stupid when it comes to your mates. You are willing to sacrifice everything."

Veral's eyes narrowed, but he refused to speak. What a pirate would never understand is that there was nothing without his mate. Despite all the rumors about his species, he was grateful that outsiders knew so little about the particulars of their society, especially their mate bonds.

Not knowing that he would follow her in death kept the male operating within the letter of the agreement out of fear of retaliation.

His eyes followed the pirate captain as the male left the room. When he was out of sight, Veral gave one last cursory glance around the space, his eyes falling on the outline of a door. That had to lead to a small, private room. Making note of it, Veral grunted and spun around as he followed the captain back out to the main area of the wreckage where the crew was congregated.

"Alien tech reacts to our systems," he fired off to Kaylar as his gaze studied the pirates shoving by each other as they fought for rations.

"Is it controllable?"

"Debatable. Links drops out if not touched directly. A direct pathway link could be established, I believe, with time."

"And the tech?"

"As of yet, no prognosis can be made as to what might be useful against the pirate until we arrive at the main wreckage."

"Very well. Keep me informed," Kaylar grumbled as he signed off.

Veral lingered at the far end of the crowd, his eyes following Terri as she settled in a vacant spot closest to the wall. The youngling sat by her side, his lips pressed together in a grimace of pain as she wrapped a clean leaf tightly around his hand. The leaf would hold for the night, but as soon as the pirates were asleep, he was going to bring her to the medical bay. He needed the contact with her, for however little time they had. In the morning, she could change the leaf out for clean bandages.

Leaning against the wall, he watched and waited.

14

Terri frowned down at Garswal's wound as she wrapped it with the clean fibrous leaf that Azan had provided her. The bite was shallow and hadn't shown any sign of envenomation, but there was still a chance if left open it could get infected.

"How did this happen again?" she asked, tucking the leaf tightly closed.

The boy sighed. "I was cutting away a vine and this creature with a long body, a flat head, and many legs fell from the tree onto my hand. I tried to shake it off, but it bit me."

She grimaced at the description. It sounded a lot like an insect. She hated most of the ones that crawled through the desert. Scorpions, centipedes… They all could have suffered a fiery death as far as she was concerned. She had dealt with enough scorpion stings that she was fairly certain of what to look for, but she would check the bandage first thing in the morning, just in case, and clean it. It would mean more of their water supply since the pirates weren't keen on sharing, but she didn't want to risk his hand.

Sighing, she patted his hand gently before releasing it. "I think you'll be all right. Go get some rations before there's nothing left."

Garswal brightened and with a nod of his head shot to his feet and disappeared among the stampede of males vying for what there was. Azan pushed away from the wall.

"I think I will go make sure that he doesn't get trampled by that lot. I will bring you back something if you will be all right sitting here by yourself for a few minutes."

Terri waved the female off. "I'm fine here. I doubt anyone will try anything."

Azan gave her a doubtful look but disappeared after Garswal, giving Terri a precious moment of solitude while everyone was distracted. Her hand slipped to her shoulder and attempted to knead out the tension. She nearly yelped with a hand closed around the base of her neck and began to gently rub.

Tension drained out of her almost immediately when she recognized Veral's touch as he hummed to her, his mandibles vibrating with the occasional soft click. The sound was as soothing as his touch. Terri leaned against him, smiling.

"I've missed you," she murmured.

"I know, as I have you. It will not be much longer, anastha."

Her eyebrows arched as she cast a glance at the male crouching at her side.

"Not much longer until what?"

His lips parted as if to speak, but he hesitated until his mouth clamped back down into a determined line. He shook his head. "It is better if you do not know. Not yet. There will be less risk to you."

"In case you've missed it, this isn't exactly a party here," she hissed.

"I have noticed. Be strong, anastha. I will come for you tonight."

His lips brushed over the top of her head, followed by the

drag of his mandibles before he retreated so quickly from her side that she almost wondered if she imagined him there. Her eyes scanned the crowd, catching only glimpses of his dark form until he completely disappeared.

"You look pensive," Azan said conversationally as she sat at Terri's side, catching her off guard.

Terri dredged up a smile as the female narrowed her eyes on her suspiciously. As much as she wanted to confide her worries to the Blaithari, she couldn't forget that the female couldn't truly be her friend. The circumstances made them odd companions for the time being. She wouldn't risk saying anything that could potentially put any sort of suspicion on Veral, so she shook her head and accepted the pair of ration bars that were handed to her.

"It's nothing. Daydreaming, I guess. I miss my mate." That much at least she felt safe to confess. It was a normal reaction.

Azan's expression closed, but her lips pressed together as if thinking of something unpleasant. She sighed and took a large bite of ration bar. "A good reason to never take a mate. It makes you dependent on them. Even for those who are not weak, it still makes one vulnerable. Out here, being vulnerable to any kind of personal attachments is dangerous."

"You miss out on a lot though," Terri said quietly.

The female beside her snorted. "And what would that be? Someone hoarding all of the bedding? A male who snores so loudly that it is impossible to sleep? Or would it be the bossy male who demands that you follow his every whim—all for your own good of course? No. By myself is far preferable."

"What of someone to love you? To be strong so that sometimes you can be allowed to feel weak and remind yourself that you need someone other than yourself? A companion in life, someone who'll bring you the heads of your enemies as love tokens," she threw out there, recalling Veral's attempt to do just that when he was courting her.

"Then I will save my credits to purchase a great northern vingnol," Azan snorted mirthfully.

"Do I want to know what that is?" Terri asked, amusement creeping into her voice.

The pirate leaned in close, her eyes sparkling with laughter. "It is a domesticated companion animal for hunting and other tasks. It has eight legs, and its body stands as high as my waist. They have huge squared heads with three eyes and four prominent fangs among a great many sharp teeth. Generally, they possess nasty dispositions to everyone including their masters. But they are loyal and make excellent bedwarmers once you get past the drool. Absolutely lovely breed," she chuckled.

Terri slapped a hand over her mouth to muffle to unexpected laughter that bubbled out of her. "That sounds absolutely horrific," she chortled around her fingers.

Azan smirked. "Says the female who has a rabid monster trying to chew its way through the *metal door* of her quarters."

"Krono is great… He just doesn't deal well with being locked in—or locked out, for that matter."

She tried to think of an intimate moment that she and Veral had that didn't involve Krono lying somewhere in the room. Not one came to mind, except when the dorashnal had be put out at night while strangers were on the ship. Even then, he hated being shut out and had snarled and attempted to get through the door more than once when he got tired of sniffing through the corridors.

"Maybe he needs a mate," Terri muttered to herself.

"Ah, you want two insane males on your salvager then—or are you hoping that regular fucking will calm him down? I hate to tell you, but it is rarely the case in males who I have personally know," Azan observed.

"The males in the crew talk about needing to fuck all the

time," Garswal piped up from where he sat at Azan's other side, steadily devouring his rations.

Terri nearly choked on her food. She hadn't seen him there and had forgotten that he was there, likely listening as they talked.

"You are right," Azan agreed, casting the boy a grin. "Most grown males have only one thing on their mind and little sense besides. Those who have brains tend to be pretty awful. Not you, though. You will be too intelligent for all of that," she said, patting him on the head.

His smile in reply was so wide it nearly split his face as he devoured the last of his rations. He then proceeded to eat half a ration that Azan and Terri each gave him. Seeing him in such good spirits, and obviously not bothered by the bite on his hand, eased her concerns.

She still hated that Egbor had put him in that situation and was likely going to do it again tomorrow.

Brushing the crumbs from her hands, Terri pulled out her ponytail to finger comb the unwashed length. Although the quarters provided for her on the pirate ship had a cleansing unit, she missed her own soaps and cleansers, not to mention the relaxation tub that could be summoned up from the floor and filled with hot water perfumed with whatever scent she had filled and programmed. The pirate ship didn't have the little luxuries that Veral painstakingly provided for her, like basic cleansers, but the hard spray had at least got her clean. Marching through the bogs left her desperately in need of a bath and made her think fondly on even that basic unit.

She frowned as she thought of all the credits that they were losing on this trip. She was going to have to trim the luxuries down until they got another assignment.

Though she didn't really understand how the tech worked, especially not the replicators, she understood that everything cost credits. Even Veral's salvaging served a purpose. Sometimes he sold directly to individuals who were looking for parts, sometimes it was brought in to artisans who melted it down for their creations, and sometimes salvage was taken to processing establishments that broke the matter down into its basic elements that were loaded into one of a great many tubes that went into replicators. That pretty much ruined the *magic* of the whole thing for her, but it helped to understand how what they did was important.

The fancier and more expensive the replicator, the more it could potentially do, and the greater amount of raw material those units required, because apparently the units couldn't fabricate stuff out of absolutely nothing.

Veral, because he was often in space for long periods, had an expensive one. Even then, however, he had far less of the pricey raw material tubes for creating mechanical pieces or fibers and more for creating food, which was something that they did need plenty of.

Something that they would run uncomfortably low on if they could not restock soon.

She froze at the thought, her stomach dipping as she imagined a long, miserable stretch of going hungry. Of having no credits for…well, anything. She held onto the hope that the meager amount of credits that the pirates transferred would still be waiting in their accounts. *Please let it still be in our accounts!*

15

The hand that settled on her shoulder woke Terri out of a deep sleep, her entire body jerking with surprise until another hand, warm and familiar, settled over her mouth. Her eyes searched the dark, and she relaxed as she met Veral's glowing eyes. The cybernetics under his skin faintly illuminated the darkness, but his eyes were always visible unless he covered them. She smiled against his hand as she patted his arm.

Slowly, his hand slid away from her lips as he touched a finger to his mouth in a gesture for silence. She nodded and quietly pushed up to her feet. Her mate didn't give her an opportunity to walk. Probably a good thing, since she had never mastered any form of stealth. Instead, she wrapped her arms and legs around Veral as he lifted her up and proceeded to carry her from Azan's side.

A shiver of apprehension rolled through her as they moved further away from the group. Ever since they had been captured by pirates, they hadn't even dared to be alone together.

Terri didn't say anything nor make any sign of objection. She couldn't summon the energy to care about anything more than the feel of him against her body and the soul of his heart beating beneath her ear as she rested her head against his chest.

She wasn't unobservant, however. Despite the darkness obscuring her vision, she felt the brush of a doorway against her shoulders as they entered another room. She almost thought he would put her down then, but instead he strode further until he stopped. Sweeping her arm out, she felt the cold metal wall behind her.

"Veral?" she whispered uncertainly.

"Wait," he replied softly.

The cybernetics in his hand were visible as he brought it up and set it against the wall. A light flared, and a soft sliding sound met her ears as a musty scent filled the air. He had opened... something. She nearly squeaked in surprise when Veral started walking again without warning—into the wall.

A room!

The wall whispered as it shut behind them. It was only then that Veral gently set her on her feet. He detached a disc from the shoulder of his armor and pressed the top of it. A soft blue light started up in its center, growing steadily brighter until the entire lamp glowed, lighting up the room.

Unlike the rest of the ship, this room had random personal items scattered throughout—literally. Shelves had fallen over, dumping their contents on the floor, and a utilitarian table lay on its side just in front of what looked like a cushioned platform for resting. Everything else was a litter of broken items spread on the floor.

"What is this?" she murmured.

"It is just off the medical bay. The logical conclusion would be that it was the doctor's private office. Where, apparently, he also must have slept at times," he added.

Terri slowly turned to face her mate, her eyebrows going up. "Slept, huh? Did you bring me in here for sleep, Veral?"

"Impossible," he growled unhappily. "As much as I want you with me, it cannot be risked. I just needed some time."

Terri ran her hands over his broad chest, concealed beneath his armor. She understood how he felt. It seemed as if time served their enemies, striving to keep them apart. A stolen moment or two to enjoy even the briefest of contact was worth it. Despite how much she tried to stay optimistic that they would get out of everything fine once the pirates got what they wanted, she wasn't so naïve as to believe that there wasn't an equally good chance that they wouldn't be walking away from the remains of the *Evandra*.

If this was possibly her last opportunity to touch and share her love with her mate, then she wasn't going to pass it up.

She knew that he felt the same. She heard it in his fervently whispered praises as he peeled her armor from her body. Every word reverent, making her aware of just how much he needed her and treasured her presence in his life. He wasn't as skilled with words as a poet, but the honesty in what he spoke moved her heart.

"Perfection," he hissed as he gazed upon her. "I would kill all of them for you and lay them vanquished at your feet that you would be adorned in the glory of the blood I shed in your honor. Never has a mate been more deserving of such honors."

"Fuck, I love it when you promise to do horrific things to my enemies," she whispered as she slid her hands over his taut pectorals.

"I would feed you delicacies from their bones."

"Okay, a little much there… but I can get definitely get down with feeding me. In all ways. Gods, I need you," she ground out as her hands continued their upward movement.

A low rumble met her touch, and his eyes slid shut with pleasure as she slowly ran her hand up to the tab at his collar that sealed his armor. Pressing it, she hummed with delight as the material split beneath her hand, falling away from the dark silver scales of her mate's chest.

"Anastha," he hissed as her hands trailed down his body to cup the swollen sack that his cock—rather, his civix—rested inside.

At the pressure of her hands, his dark civix slipped out in a rush. It was so thick that she couldn't even close her fingers around it. It slipped and writhed in her grasp, the hook at its tip twitching as the tiny tubes that ran up the length of his sex began to drizzle lubricant into her hand. Veral's face pinched, his hips twitching with need.

She began to drop to her knees, wanting to taste him on her tongue and drive him crazy with her mouth, but his hands on her arms tightened, stopping her. Instead, he drew her closer until her bare chest was plastered against his, his vibrissae vibrating and twitching as they coiled against her breasts, along her neck, and into her hair.

All of her attention, however, was fastened on his hotly glowing eyes as his head dropped and his lips claimed hers.

The feel of his two tongues invading her mouth sent a bolt of desire punching through her. She sank into him, her single tongue tussling eagerly with his slender pair. As her arms twined around his neck and his vibrissae clung to her, their bodies slid together, simulating the instinctive movements of mating. His hands dropped, sliding down her sides to cup possessively for a moment over her still flat belly before sliding down to the back of her thighs. With one swift movement, he yanked her up into his arms and walked to the edge of the sleeping platform.

Holding her firmly against him, he slid onto the bed. Though the movement kicked up clouds of dust, neither of them paid any attention to it. They were far more interested in the contact points between their bodies that had been touch-starved for days since their separation. Terri could feel the energy between them, that connection of their bond, practically hum with intensity as they grew increasingly frantic.

At some point, her legs crept around his hips, pulling him tightly against her until they were pelvis to pelvis. Veral's back arched to maintain their kisses despite their height discrepancy. At the contact of his civix gliding along her sex, a shudder ran through her, and Terri gasped into his mouth. He pressed tighter to her, swallowing every sound that she made, muffling it so that they wouldn't be discovered.

His sex slid against hers several times, flicking her clit with each pass until she was jerking her hips against him in a silent plea, her arousal a slick coating on her pussy and the inside of her upper thighs. He pulled back, looking down at her, eyes hooded with desire. His lips parted, the tips of his tongues pushing through as the tip of his cock notched at her opened. With a jerk of his hips, he slid deep within her.

Terri's hips rose to meet him, a strangled sound barely escaping her throat as she felt his civix glide and twist within her as he began to move. He clutched her ass at an angle off the bed as he drove into her with every snap of his hips. Dazed, she watched as his large body moved gracefully above hers, the muscles in his jaw tensing with effort as he picked up into a hard rut, his mandibles slowly stretching wider as his breaths puffed from his lips in eager pants.

It took everything she had to cling to him, her body tightening as tiny tremors began to quake through her. Her muscles instinctively tightened around him, needing more, her fingers tangling among his vibrissae, gripping them as she dug her heels into his ass, her hips jerking frantically as she rode the rapid rise to her peak.

She was aware of the exact moment that Veral's flexible hook scraped and caught hold, his cock swelling rapidly. A scream tore from her, muffled once more by his mouth as he ground into her, his own hips shuttling in a broken tempo until he snarled against her mouth. His release broke from him as hot seed splashed deep within her. His breath left him in ragged pants punctuated by growls and snarls with every twitch of his cock as it continued to release until he dropped onto his elbows, his body spent.

As she lay there beneath him, Terri's stroked his back, relishing the feel of his hard muscles and slick scales beneath her palms. A soft trill vibrated in his throat as he nuzzled her. Everything was so perfect that she could almost forget there was a group of murderous pirates waiting for them.

Everything that mattered was within that moment.

A sigh left her as she snuggled her cheek against him. "I don't want this moment to ever end."

"That is a peculiar thing to say."

"It means that in this moment I'm happy and hate for it to end and go back to the shit that's been going on."

"Anastha, we will survive it. I would rather go through the struggle with you at my side than be locked in an eternal moment where everything that we are ceases to exist. I do not wish for this moment to continue forever, but to have many years to find thousands of new moments."

A soft laugh left her as she brushed her nose against his scales. "How is it that whenever it sounds like you're going to be all cold and clinical, you can still say the strangest and yet most romantic things?"

"Perhaps because humans are a strange species. I was not speaking romantically. I do not understand how one endeavors to be romantic. I only relay simple truths to you, anastha."

"You call my species strange but offer to leave body parts as love tokens," she said.

"That is a logical gesture. There is no greater show of devotion that a willingness to fight for your mate and vanquish their foes. It reinforces the uniting of the family unit and demonstrates the male to be a fit caretaker for his family."

"And what about your females? Do they promise to slay your enemies?" she teased.

He paused, his head tilting as he considered. "There have been a few known occasions when a female has bested the enemy of her male. This is especially the case in our most ancient legends which speak of powerful females of great skill and cunning who attempt to secure males for themselves. The only thing that saves the male is the strength of his mate standing up to the sorceress."

Terri's brows winged up at that. "You're this great, advanced civilization—and you have sorceresses?"

Her mate frowned down at her. "They are legends from different times, not to be taken as factual but to glorify our ancestresses who were willing to match wits to help their mates vanquish their enemies. It was because of the first legend, the story of Emnawalath and her mate Etmangoluvarthi, that the males make their oaths, for it was the oath he made to her when she gave everything to him. Although we do not expect our females to vanquish our enemies, we still give the oath to acknowledge that they are sacrificing to open their household to accept their mate that he might join her family." He dropped his head, his lips grazing her jaw. "You deserve no less honors—you who have given up more than most Argurma females to be mine."

"Yeah, well, it was a pretty good trade, I think," she replied softly. "I left a pretty miserable life to have one in the stars with my big mate. I wouldn't make any other decision."

He paused, an uncertainty flashing over his face. "You have been restless and less happy of late. It has been distressing."

Terri glanced away to hide her guilt. "I haven't been unhappy… just… unable to find where I fit in. You're so determined to protect me that you keep me away from everything, and suddenly it feels like I'm no longer living. This is the most living

I've really done since the incident on the space station. This wasn't how I thought it was going to be... but I also understand. Azan made me realize that you've had to protect me. I'm not strong enough."

His eyes closed, his expression pained before he opened them again. "Anastha, you are strong. Too strong. It makes me worry that others will attempt to hurt you and take you away from me."

"And physically too weak to defend myself. You can say it, Veral. I know it's the truth."

"I dislike this truth more than any other," he muttered, his tone laced with resentment. "I do not wish my mate to fear or experience pain. But I do not wish to snuff out your joy."

"Yeah." She sighed. "This human stuff kinda sucks when it comes to playing out in the universe."

"I will protect you," he growled.

"And I love that, but I need to protect me too. Especially when we have our baby. I have to be able to protect them and myself if, for whatever reason, you're not there. I can't be helpless when we have a baby to care for."

A long, ragged sigh escaped him, and he nodded. "We will find an answer."

16

Veral did not want to let her go, but as the hour grew later, he knew he had no choice. His civix retreated back into his sheath, and eventually he forced his arms to release his mate. Sitting on the bed, he watched sadly as she also sat up.

She had used a scrap of cloth she found to wipe between her legs and was now bending to pick up her armor. Soon they would return to the other room, where danger would constantly surround her once more. He would have to sneak her by the males on guard and leave her with nothing more for protection than the fierce female Blaithari.

He hated to give that up to her. Everything in him protested.

He should be the one protecting and caring for his mate, not watching from afar while another did it. It made him feel dishonored and the mate bond distressed, though he knew that much was largely within his mind. To his instincts, Azan was an unwelcome intruder.

"Oww! What the fuck?" Terri shrieked as she jerked her right hand up to her chest, her left clamped tightly over it.

He rose to his feet and leaped over the bed, his sensors scanning as he searched for the threat. "What is it?"

Something scurried among the debris, circling around. Veral yanked Terri into his arms, a snarl vibrating in his chest as he tracked the movement. The energy signature coming from it was not organic. It was similar to that of the Elshavan uplinks.

He froze in surprise. What could possibly still be operational after all that time?

"Something under the bed clawed me," she hissed out in pain. "What the hell was it?"

She pulled away her left hand to look at the blood beading on the cut and dripping down her wrist. Veral growled and pulled her toward him, his senses extended as his systems collected the surrounding information and his vibrissae twisted anxiously around him.

It was slipping through the rubble, drawing closer. Veral's vibrissae rattled, a low hiss rising in his throat as the thing zigzagged. It moved almost as if it had a sort of program designed to mimic intelligence as it stalked closer. He watched it warily, tracking its every movement. It seemed to move farther away, but at the last minute it turned and rushed toward Terri. As it leaped in the air, its long metallic fibers extending wide from a brilliantly green body, Veral whipped his hand through the air, the small horn on his wrist catching it and dashing it to the ground.

Terri hopped back with a squeak of alarm as the spindly fibers whipped through the air. The ends were needle sharp, more than effective for piercing through vulnerable tissue. Especially on a species such as a human whose skin had no natural defenses against it. It would have a harder time against his scales.

"Fuck!" she cursed as she crawled back away from it. "What the hell is it?"

Veral's eyes narrowed on the tech before he brought his boot down sharply upon it, the loud crunch of components snapping filling the silence of the room. Lifting his foot away, he cocked his head and looked down at the crushed red body of tech. Tiny sparks lit across it as its "legs" twitched uselessly.

Terri scooted forward as he lifted his eyes and scanned for any signs of more of the things. He couldn't detect anything, but he was disturbed to acknowledge the fact that not sensing meant nothing if he had a difficult time connecting with the unfamiliar energy signature.

It had felt oddly like bio-tech. There had been a few attempts to make something like that among his species with the idea to upgrade and eventually replace their current tech with something more fully integrated, but nothing successful.

"It's like some sort of mechanical bug... but not," Terri marveled as she stared at it. "I wonder what it was trying to do."

Veral shook his head, his fingers curling around her arm as he pulled her away. The thing had intentionally drawn her blood, but he could not understand for what purpose. There wasn't a trace of it within the mechanisms when he crushed it, so it did not appear to be attempting to store it. His eyes inspected the room, his vibrissae rattling as they vibrated while he attempted to get another read on the environment.

The room that had seemed as a welcome sanctuary only moments before, he could only now see as hostile.

The upended table with components strewn around it made him tug his mate further back. There were parts that looked similar to the bio-tech he just terminated. The medic was working on something—an experiment perhaps. He would not remain in this room with his mate for a moment longer. Dropping down, he retrieved her armor and searched it thoroughly for any other signs of bio-tech. Only when he was satisfied that it was clean did he hand it back to her.

Terri was silent as she slipped the armor back on and said nothing further when he lifted her up into his arms and carried her from the room. He would go back and investigate later, to see if there was anything worth discovering about the tech, and in case there was something she had been exposed to. But now, he would get his mate to safety.

As safe as she could be surrounded by murdering pirates. It was ironic just how quickly the situation changed with this new development.

On their way through the medical bay, he set her down to activate a storage area that had bandages. Tearing a segment off, he wrapped it around her hand before pressing the torn end down against the surface beneath his thumb to hold it in place while he searched for a binding.

Terri shifted her hand beneath his. "Uh, Veral, I think the end is sticking down."

Glancing at her hand, he removed his thumb and noted that the torn end had completely sealed against the wrapped bandaging. He gave it a light tug to make sure that it would not loosen and nodded in satisfaction. That was practical. Without comment, he handed her what was left of the bandaging and swung her back up into his arms.

Focusing on keeping his footsteps light, he moved silently among the crew. Due to the safety of the enclosed wreckage, those who were awake and on guard were fewer, and were focused solely on the forest.

No one noticed that he carried his mate back to Azan's side.

As he set her down. Terri's hand tangled in his vibrissae, drawing his head down to press her lips against his. It was a silent communication of feeling, and Veral embraced it as he deepened the kiss, drawing his tongues along hers until they were both nearly breathless. He ignored the pang of regret and longing as he pulled away.

Not surprisingly, at that moment, Azan stirred, her yellow eyes opening. Her hand went immediately to her blaster her as her body tensed with hostility. Veral stilled, prepared to defend his mate, but the tension fled her as her eyes met his. Her gaze slid to Terri for a moment before returning to him, a smirk curving her lips as her nostrils flared. He knew exactly what she was scenting for, and he bared his teeth at her intrusion.

Although Blaithari night vision was not as good as many species, and nowhere near the cybernetic-enhanced vision of the Argurma, it was far better than that of humans. There was still enough glow from the embers that she had no trouble seeing his expression. She sketched him a small salute and turned away to give him his last moment of privacy with Terri as he prepared to leave.

He snorted in exasperation at the pirate before turning his attention back to his mate, his hand stroking her cheek. She leaned into his touch. It was only a moment, gone when he stepped away, but that moment was everything. This night would have to sustain them over the lonely nights ahead.

Be strong, be safe, he wanted to tell her. Instead, he turned away and left her.

He did not turn and look back to watch her settle once more at Azan's side. He was not strong enough. It was too tempting to pick his mate up and run back for their ship, even knowing that the pirate ship orbiting the planet would shoot them down.

His efforts were better spent returning to that room to look for more clues about the thing that attacked Terri. How many more bio-techs had the Elshavan devised, and was there possibly worse awaiting for them on the *Evandra*?

The thought chilled his blood and sent alarms through his systems.

Returning to the room, Veral righted the table and searched among the debris until he found what appeared to be a private data recorder. He touched his hand to the back but was less disconcerted this time at the uplink that burrowed into his systems as he held the recorder.

There was always a probability that the device would be code locked. Fortunately, that was not the case. The screen flared on and he tilted his head curiously as an image of a strange male stared back at him on the screen.

Like Terri, he had soft skin, though there was a subtle scaling on it, nothing that would significantly protect him from outside damage. Long, fine, oily hair coiled in braids as it hung around his face, heavy with ornaments clamped in several places. There was possibly a meaning to the ornaments that would have intrigued Terri, but Veral was more curious about the firm, anxious look to the male's expression.

His finger slid over the image. It flickered out to reveal an empty workstation lit up with numerous wired parts of bio-tech like the one he had crushed, and others that appeared to be different types in varying stages of completion.

The male dropped down in front of the screen and swept his hands over his face, rubbing at his eyes in a show of exhaustion. Leaning forward, he began to speak in a low, sibilant voice. Thanks to the existing records that he had been poring over, Veral's translator picked up the language quickly.

"For once, I am thankful that this room is soundproof and no one else on my staff is able to hear what I am about to say. I have been suspicious for a while as to what exactly our purpose is on the Evandra. *The prince tells us little and keeps the vast number of scientists separated and out of communication with one another. But something is not right. There are things loose in this ship. Tech of the like that is not cataloged, seemingly entirely experimental in design. A whole wing of scientists died, and then another. I have been delaying my own assignments on the melgadinal to focus on something that will be useful to protect us from our creations. The melgadinal is a mistake, an aberration. We have successfully grown a fetus of a monster that is born with tech that advances and restructures itself as it grows larger at an*

accelerated rate, as I have been instructed by command. They are one of what I suspect may be many ongoing experiments that we are told will wipe the Diralthax out of existence so they never threaten our people again. But they have turned on us."

The male swiped a hand over his face again as the screen showed schematics demonstrating how the symbiont would join with its host.

"I do not know if my creations will be successful, but I am uploading all my data in case we fail. The gymotakin symbiotic armor… I do not have time to accurately test it. These things cannot be brought down by blasters. The creatures metabolize energy blasts. I think I have calculated correctly. At least I hope so… I—What is that?"

He turned, his eyes scanning the room behind him. Solemnly, he turned back to the recorder.

"If we do not resolve this situation, I fear it will be the end of the Evandra*, and anyone who finds her. I pray to the gods that, if we fail, no one ever discovers our location."*

The scientist gasped as the room shook around him, and the recording cut out. Though there was nothing to suggest what had happened, Veral systems pricked with alarm. Whatever had been loose on the Evandra had brought the ship down and killed the crew.

Staring at the black screen, a sense of apprehension filled him as he downloaded the content from the recorder. The files were badly fragmented in places, but the bits that he was able to recover provided a glimpse into the research that had been underway, as well as information on the gymotakin symbionts.

The symbiotic armor was fascinating, but the plans for the bio-tech experiment that the scientist had been working on made him still in horror at the unnatural utilization of the tech. It wasn't augmentations, like the Argurma focused on. No, it was an entirely bio-engineered creature made of bio-metal, with a heightened predatory AI designed to search and destroy its targets like an unnatural creation of night terrors.

It was a monstrosity that never should have existed.

That the AI likely malfunctioned and sent the creatures on a killing spree through the ship made any salvage of the *Evandra* untenable. Suddenly, finding the resting place of the ship was the last thing Veral wanted to do, but there was only so long he could delay the captain. Egbor was vain, but he was not a fool. He would notice if they were not drawing any closer to the wreckage on the schematic.

He hissed angrily. If he could not convince the captain, he had no choice but to take his mate to the *Evandra* and hope that Kaylar arrived before anything else noticed their arrival.

"Kaylar, increase your rate of speed."

"As you know, increasing speed beyond safety limits is highly dangerous and not..."

Veral snarled impatiently and transmitted his visual recording and the downloaded files. Silence fell as he waited for Kaylar to open the files.

"Data received. I will be there in sixty-five standard galactic hours."

Nearly three standard rotations early. It would have to suffice.

17

Terri stirred, her brow furrowing. It couldn't be time to wake up already. Something was tickling her nose. She groaned and swiped her hand at her face to brush whatever it was away. It moved away, and she grumbled unhappily. She hated when Azan messed with her while she was sleeping.

Something touched the bridge of her nose again.

"Azan knock it off, already," she mumbled, slapping at whatever the pirate was tormenting her with.

It moved, and a weight landed on her head. *What the…?* Her eyes opened, and she squinted at her hand in the dark. A soft green glow illuminated her hand, and her breath stuttered in panic as it scurried up her wrist.

No, no… *No!*

With a shriek, Terri jerked up, stumbling to her feet as she whipped her arm around, trying to dislodge it as it scurried beneath the opening in her armor at the wrist. A hair-raising scream left her, her fingers digging at her sleeve, attempting to push it back out from beneath it.

It's not working!

Her breath came out in ragged pants as terror coursed through her. Giving up on trying to push it out, she slammed her wrist against the wall, hoping that would crush it.

She could hear Veral's panicked roar, but it sounded faint, distant. The sound that was more immediate was the one that came from the pirates leaping up, shouting out in alarm, pistols and blades drawn as they looked around for a sign of danger. She ignored them all as she cried and slammed her hand repeatedly on the wall.

Terri didn't care if everyone saw her blubbering like a baby. She was justified in losing her shit as she frantically attempted to get that thing off her arm.

Pain pierced her forearm just as Azan shoved her firmly against the wall. The pirate's scales were dull and pale pink. As one pair of arms held Terri in place, another pair yanked her arm forward, stretching it out. Terri was distantly aware of Veral shoving his way through the gathering crowd, his hard snarls threatening males who had leveled blasters at her. Azan pushed up the flexible sleeve of her armor, and they both gasped in horror as numerous tendrils whipped out from the body of the bio-tech. Blood flowed around its body as its primary legs assisted it as it burrowed into her forearm.

"What in the name of the gods is that!?" Azan shouted. "Cursed shit of all things profane! I am going to try to dig it out." Yellow eyes met brown, the female's pinprick pupils dilating with emotion until they were clearly visible black sideways ovals. She yanked out her dagger and placed the tip at the side of the glowing green body. The tendrils were flowing around her forearm, jabbing into her and sinking into her.

"Please..." Terri said. "Get it off of me."

A spurt of blood appeared at the side of the blade seconds before a dark hand spun out and knocked the dagger away. Azan hissed as the clatter of metal hitting metal echoed through the room.

"Do not," Veral snarled as his face lowered threateningly. "Can you not see that it has fully attached itself into her arm? It is a symbiont. Bio-tech created by the Elshavan."

"What is a symbiont?" snarled an Igwin.

"A parasite," Azan returned, her lip curling at it.

Terri was half amused to note that, for once, an Igwin looked at her warily rather than with the usual carnal hunger. It was a refreshing change. In fact, all the Igwins were drawing away from her. Hysterically, Terri wondered if alien tech suddenly made her foul to them.

Well, good. That was one good thing to come from the crap ton of pain.

"A tech symbiont is different. Its programming drives it to link to a type of being it has been engineered to recognize. The Elshavan, though they have scales, have a softer appearance like my mate. In order to fulfill its purpose, it must do as it is programmed to do. At this point, now that the merger is complete and it has joined to her body, it is nothing more than a tool that she must learn to use. One that cannot be removed without irreversible damage to her body. Tech implants are not to be trifled with except by experts in the field, and only in dire emergencies. Some Argurma weapons operate it in this fashion, though they lack the obvious sophistication of the bio-tech that has bonded to my female. One thing would be noticeably the same, however. It cannot be removed."

"For what purpose was it created?" Egbor asked as he pushed through the crowd. His pistol was still primed in his hand, but it hung lax at his side rather than pointed at her. "Will it harm us? Or do you think it might be valuable?" Greed lit his eyes as his tongue swept over his lips hungrily.

Terri instinctively wanted to tuck her arm out of sight before he got an idea to attempt to hack it off.

Veral frowned and shook his head. "I do not know if it would have any value since we do not know yet exactly what it does. Even so, given the way that it has bonded to her, if you did remove it, you would end up damaging it in addition to killing her. For anyone else, it is just a bit of metal and biological material. I do not think it will harm anyone in the crew as it is now a part of her. I found a lab, and from what I understand, a scientist designed the tech to protect against something far worse."

"What can possibly be worse than *that*?!" a pirate shouted, gesturing to Terri's exposed arm.

She grimaced. It wasn't pretty.

Blood still seeped around the green body of the symbiont, though it was slowing as if the thing was working with her nanos to speed up her already accelerated healing. Despite the slowing trickle of blood, the skin was still swollen and flushed a painful red. What was more alarming might have been the weird green fluid that dripped out along with her blood, and the fact that her arm felt like it was on fire, the pain spreading upwards. Around the imbedded symbiont, tiny tendrils of green light could almost be seen flashing under her skin like a spiderweb of metallic veins.

Veral brushed Azan aside, and the female reluctantly moved away, giving Terri's mate full access to her. His claws were still out, betraying the lingering heights of his anxiety as he lightly touched the symbiont with his claw.

He frowned and brought his claw up and slashed down at it. Terri's entire body tensed with horror, but even as he brought his hand down, the symbiont exploded into action. Several tendrils shot up, weaving rapidly into a pair of barbed whips that slashed at her mate. He only just barely moved out of the way on time, his lips pressing into a thin slash of concentration.

What in the holy fuck *was that?*

The corner of his mouth turned up, his mandibles vibrating in a soft hum as he let out a sharp trill. The asshole was utterly delighted that the thing attached to her just attempted to flay him.

Terri's mouth dropped open as his claws retracted, and he nodded with satisfaction.

"You did that on purpose! Are you fucking *insane?*" she shouted.

Veral leaned forward and brushed his nose against her jaw, his mandibles caressing the sides of her neck in a show of affection, stepping away before it occurred to Egbor that they were breaking his precious rules.

"It was a calculated risk. I suspected that it would seek to protect you even when not summoned if a direct attack was made."

"As sickeningly sweet as this all is," the captain interrupted, "you still have not explained just what exactly it is meant to have protected them from."

Veral's lips parted, his brow furrowed. She knew this look. He was attempting to put together a reasonable reply that the pirates would understand when a horrible, screeching roar blasted over the wreckage. The sound was hollow like air blowing through a mechanical tube, and yet with all the ferocity of something very big, and very angry.

Egbor turned around as everyone slowly faced the gaping hole in the side of the wreckage. A head suddenly dropped down, its wide, shovel-like mouth parting, revealing rows upon rows of jagged metal teeth. A large violet eye, glowing with small threads of light, peered at them as it let out a terrible hiss.

As it leaned forward, a large metallic hand descended, flattening against the ground. Although it had the appearance of a matte metal, Terri could see veins and musculature, as if it were living flesh. Like something organic, but made entirely of metal. Its claws extended farther, tearing up the dirt as it dropped its head lower. A long silver tongue whipped through the opening to curl around the nearest pirate before he could gain any distance from it.

The tongue didn't just wrap around the male, but the tip stabbed into the struggling Igwin's abdomen. His mouth gaped open, his screams echoing. The tongue pulsed like a muscle, and Terri watched as his belly caved in and his skin shriveled over his frame. The male didn't move anymore at that point, hanging limp, his eyes staring out lifelessly as the monster's tongue snapped back, drawing his body into the enormous waiting mouth.

Veral pushed her back behind him, moving her deeper into the ship as the pirates fled from the creature lurking at the gap in the wall. "I believe that may be one of the things that were created on the *Evandra*."

"Oh my fucking gods," Terri whispered. "They were creating monsters."

"Engineering the perfect war machines," he observed.

"But why create something like this?"

Claws scraped at the opening, the metal screeching in protest. The metal folded back a little where it was weakest, but otherwise held.

"Because it would bring certain death," Veral hissed. He turned to address the captain. "As far as I can tell, this particular tech organism requires nocturnal conditions that it would be programmed to *hunt* during. We happened to be within its territory during its active time and it scented our presence. We are fortunate that we found shelter in something that deters it from killing us. This gives us time until sunrise. If we remain where we are until then, it will depart. I must insist that we take that opportunity to return to the ship and abandon our mission."

Egbor's head jerked up in surprise as he turned from the creature to stare in disbelief at Veral. "But you just said it will leave the area before sunrise. It is only another rotation or two until we arrive at the crash site."

"And there will be more of its kind—or worse—and we may not be so fortunate next time. According to the scientist's records

I found there were many such experiments that he suspected got loose on the starship. The closer we get to *Evandra*, the more of these bio-techs we will discover. Death waits for us at the wreckage. Nothing more."

"I disagree," the captain said coolly. His face broke into an excited smile as he rounded on his crew. "Just think! If they are creating things such as these, then they must be protecting even greater wealth than suspected on *Evandra*. Can you imagine the treasures that these guardians must oversee?" He turned his head and fixed Veral with a smile as the pirates murmured uncertainly around him. "And we have little to fear with a legendary Argurma warrior and expert salvager leading the way. These would be the kind of potentials he would have trained for."

Veral's face clouded with fury. "There is a good possibility that if you do this, you will be sentencing my mate to death."

"If you do your job well, that should not be a concern. Besides, does she not have protection now? And Azan as well. She is better protected than all of us."

Her mate stalked forward. "And what makes you think that I will not kill you now if she is so protected?"

The pirate met the obvious threat with a knowing smirk. "Because we all know that, while that symbiont is impressive, it is doubtful that even it can stop a blaster shot, or several, directly to the head... Azan."

Terri felt the nudge of metal at the back of her head followed by an instinctive surge of fear. Desperately, she wiggled her fingers, trying to get the symbiont to react and protect her.

Nothing.

Fuck! Why couldn't the tech just have a magical on switch? How the hell was this going to be of any use to her?

"I am sorry," Azan whispered regretfully. Veral's furious snarl almost drowned out the female's words as he stiffened, his vibrissae rattling as he began to turn toward them. It was only the firing up of her blaster that made him halt.

"I know. And if he kills you, I'm sorry too."

"Fair enough," Azan replied.

"It seems her tech does not immediately recognize the threat of a blaster. Must not have been in its programming. A pity. All for the best," Egbor continued. "I am sure you are also aware that my ship will still not hesitate to shoot you down before you even manage to leave the atmosphere. With this in mind, I would not react foolishly if I were you. Nothing has changed. You are still very much under my control."

"As you say," Veral growled. "I will remember this moment on the day I tear you apart with my claws."

"I suspect you might, if you had such an opportunity," the pirate agreed with a tight smile. "For now, however, you defer to me. Now get some rest, everyone. We move out at sunrise."

18

As calculated, the creature departed just before the first rays of light filtered down through the canopy. No one had been able to sleep after the attack. Although it had made it difficult for Veral to pick off another male from the group, the creature had managed to kill two males.

A reasonable trade.

It did not escape his notice that the planet was doing most of his work for him when it came to thinning the crew. So much so that, as they continued to trek further into the forest, he abandoned all immediate plans to kill the males.

Statistically, it was logical to keep what was left of the crew alive so there were extra bodies between Terri and anything else that might hunt them. Even armed with a symbiont that would likely react to the presence of the creatures, despite her current lack of skill in utilizing it, Veral wanted bodies between her and the creations of the Elshavan.

One way or another, they would all die.

The captain, however, he would particularly relish killing in slow, painful ways. He would make certain that the punishment was great enough that the male would regret even in the next world that he had forced Veral to take his mate to the *Evandra*.

The only good thing to have come from recent events was that fear of attack from the bio-tech creatures kept everyone together. That Egbor encouraged it was telling. The male did not even send Veral out to scout further ahead, wanting to keep his protection close by.

The pirate did make one concession, perhaps to ensure that Veral remained near. Other than a few stern reminders about the foolishness of taking his mate and fleeing, Veral was no longer forced to remain separate from Terri so long as the human remained close to Egbor. It provided comfort to him and reduced the continuous strain to his systems that Terri was now between him and Azan at the fore, despite the captain and his guard following close behind them.

Veral clicked to himself as he cut a quick glance at the males pushing through the thick green fronds surrounding them. Garswal stood just off to the side, the blade he carried too large in his hands, as he cut away growth at the captain's orders. His small body and blade kept most of the brush from directly touching Egbor, who peered at the wild surroundings with a distasteful curl of his lip. That male did not appreciate being out in the wilderness. It was just another thing that distinguished him from the few pirate captains Veral had known or heard of in passing.

Egbor did not willingly touch anything that had not been sterilized. The male constantly smelled of high-quality disinfectants. Even his blaster, he regularly wiped down. Though he surrounded himself by those who did the unpleasant, unclean work for him, he still managed to wield complete control over his crew.

Veral had long noted that the captain ruled not by might and ability as a pirate, but rather through cunning and manipulation alone, reinforced by a ruthlessness that kept his crew working under his orders. Keeping Veral in close proximity now was just another part of that. On a planet where they would have to battle both bio-tech creations and a local wildlife full of deadly predators, Egbor's primary concern was to assure his own safety in pursuit of the *Evandra*. He would sacrifice every one of them to accomplish his means, even if he was the only one to survive.

A movement in the path ahead zipped through his awareness along his sensory input, a reminder of the hazards that threatened them. Veral swept his arm out, knocking away the creature that stalked them in the low hanging vines with the branch he had armed himself with upon leaving their shelter.

Since the captain forbade him from having a blaster or any of the weapons utilized by the crew in concern that Veral would use it upon them, he was forced to improvise to protect his mate as they walked deeper into the forest. The thing snarled with a trembling shriek as it drew back up onto its numerous thin legs and scurried forward.

Veral's muscles tightened as his eyes tracked the predator, Terri's muttered curse close at his side as she too watched it. It raised the front of its body, its front legs spread, exposing a mouth full of hooked fangs as it let out another shriek. The front of its body was long and stick-like, providing the perfect camouflage for its bulk, despite being nearly as large as Veral's leg. The body, however, tapered down into a long, thin, prehensile tail that was also raised in the air just behind its head, the forked end jerking forward in a subtle stabbing action. Venomous barbs no doubt tipped both points of the fork.

An agitated growl left Veral's throat, his claws sliding out just as a blaster raised in the air beside him. Azan fired at the thing, the single shot hitting it amidst the tight cluster of its three eyes. Another shrill sound left it upon contact before it dropped into the dark grass surrounding it.

"Excrement-eating filth, what was *that*?" Azan snarled as she lowered her weapon.

Veral considered wresting the blaster from the female, irritated that she was the one to deal with the threat rather than himself. He did not even attempt to disguise the displeased glower that he leveled at her.

Noting his expression, the female smirked and holstered the weapon. "What is wrong, Argurma? Feeling a little... inadequate?"

Lips curling back into a snarl, he rounded on her and took a step just as Terri pressed her hands against his chest. Although he could have easily brushed by her, he yielded to his mate's touch.

That did not stop him from narrowing his eyes threateningly at the Blaithari female.

"I did not request your assistance. Your interference is a direct insult to my ability to protect my mate. Attempt to do so again, and I will merely move her to safety and allow the next predator in this forest eat you."

Azan cocked an eyebrow. "Is that so? That is not very nice."

A hard smile lit up the Blaithari's face, and while it was possibly fearsome to some beings, Veral was neither impressed nor frightened. It was nothing more than the challenge of a rival, as far as he saw it.

"I am not required to be 'nice.' My interests do not extend any further than my mate. You would do well to remember just how little my sympathies stretch beyond that. Do not get in my way again."

"Duly noted, Argurma. However, just so we are clear, you do not scare me. Nor am I inclined to jump to your pleasure. If I wish to protect the human in our company, then I will do so without seeking your permission."

Veral just barely restrained himself from snatching Terri away from the Blaithari and against the hard muscle of his body. Judging by the puzzled frown on his mate's face as she watched them, he knew that she did not understand the hostility brewing between them. It was unlikely she would approve, considering their circumstances.

It was perhaps unwise given the threat, but he did not like the female. Azan did not defer to him when it came to his mate, and he found it intolerable.

Azan's smile widened as if she could guess the exact cause of his tension. Shaking his head in an attempt to loosen the muscles and find his center of calm, his vibrissae rattling softly with the motion, he settled for a clicking snarl before turning away in dismissal.

The message was clear: she was no threat to him and no rival for his mate. She was unworthy of his concern.

He did not even glance down at the carcass lying in the thick grass at his feet. It too was no longer of concern, the details regarding the predator already filed away into his system's memory banks. Instead, he skimmed one hand down Terri's arm, her reluctance to even walk by it evident on her face and her natural recoil from it. He felt a shudder run through her. She leaned into his touch before lifting her chin and striding by it fearlessly, though she did not remove her eyes from it until it dropped out of sight.

"This planet just keeps getting better and better," she muttered. "It didn't need any help from the Elshavan to be inhabited by nightmarish wildlife."

Azan hummed in agreement at her side. "Not a planet that would make it to my list of ideal places to retire from piracy. I have never considered myself picky on that matter, so that says something."

"At least it's pretty to look at," Terri replied.

As she spoke, her fingers ran down a green vine that glittered as light hit the silvery hairs that covered it. Her hand trailed to the edge of a deep purple bloom with a diameter of nearly the same length as the whole of her arm.

A sense of foreboding prickled through Veral as his eyes fastened on the flower. He noted the serrated edge of the petals and paler spines on the bigger ones that ran down to the center of the bloom. The spines clustered thicker in throat of the flower in a manner that disturbed him.

He was not certain exactly why it distressed him until he felt a vibration of movement from the flower. His hand shot forward to grab Terri's arms the exact moment she yanked her hand back, narrowly avoiding the snap of the closing petals. His eyes fastened on her as she drew in a sharp, startled breath.

"Fuck!"

Azan made a shrill sound between her teeth as she skirted the cluster of flowering vines cautiously at great distance.

"Stay away from the flowers!" she yelled back to the crew.

There were a few incredulous snorts and some laughter, but it all cut off when a scream rose up behind them. Veral glanced back, his vibrissae rustling in surprise as one of the guards stumbled against the captain, dark blood gushing everywhere from the ragged wound where his arm had been. It splattered over the nearby fronds and leaves of the brush as he flailed.

Egbor hissed an unintelligible curse under his breath and lifted his blaster. The discharge cracked through the air as the male crumpled to the ground, his screams silenced.

The captain shook his head, and he looked down at the guard's corpse. "Brushed the damn vine in attempt to push it away from me. Good male died an honorable death."

In his peripheral vision, Veral watched as Terri's mouth dropped open, a red flush of anger rising in her cheeks.

"Bullshit! You could have avoided them if you made the attempt instead of making your lackeys clear everything in your path. It's because of you that he was injured, and you just shot him."

Veral bristled as the captain calmly pointed his blaster at Terri. His eyes glinted with warning as he addressed her coldly.

"I suggest you gain control of your tongue, female, before you wear away the last of my fond regard for you. I will not tolerate being challenged… Not by any male nor by you. Despite what you think of me, what I did was a kindness. He would have suffered greatly, and his blood would have drawn predators to us. Now should we continue on—or do you really wish to discuss this further? I can inflict so much pain without doing any true harm."

Veral stepped forward, a rattling growl releasing from him, and the blaster hummed with power as Egbor cocked a brow at him.

"Do not do anything foolish, Veral," Egbor cautioned. "If you press me, I will kill her."

"Argurma," Azan murmured.

Hissing angrily, his vibrissae rattled as information flooded his systems. He could practically taste the coiled tension and anger radiating from the male. From Azan too, although he knew it was for another reason. The other guard moved, also directing his blaster at Terri.

Veral's eyes narrowed and the captain paled slightly before recovering. Veral knew that the male saw the promise of death in their depths. This was the second time that the captain had threatened to kill her since they arrived on the planet.

He would not be leaving it alive.

"For fuck's sake," Terri snapped as she pushed between them. "You're not going to kill me just yet," she said with a hard glare at Egbor. She turned to Veral then, flattening her hands against his chest. "Later," she whispered.

Energy snapped through his muscles, every inch of him thrumming for a fight. A fight that did not come. Her touch restored his control. Instead of lunging for the pirate as he wanted, he wrapped a possessive arm around Terri, drawing her to him before pulling her around until she was in front of him, within the shelter of his body.

She was correct. Later, he would remove the male's head from his body. He would gild it in the pirate's own wealth and present it to her. She had a strange objection to such trophies, but perhaps if it were gilded it would more suitably honor her, if she disliked seeing the unadorned bone.

19

After the confrontation with the captain, there was unease among the pirates as they climbed into the higher elevation, away from the low bogs. Terri was aware of it, but kept her attention on the forest. She hadn't even been aware of the animal that Veral and Azan brought down until it was knocked to the ground directly in her path.

The forest was beautiful, but dangerous. She had no doubt that, even as it became more fantastic as they ascended into its depths and the forest became all the more glorious, there were far worse threats that lurked within it.

And it was beautiful, unlike anything she could have ever imagined existing on Earth, though she knew there were forests and great trees that once grew there, before the devastations. But in the material that she had read since acquiring the info dumps in the translator Veral implanted, nothing had been described that matched what she saw on this planet. Only those of the outer forest bore any resemblance to what she had imagined once grew on Earth. That changed as they went deeper into the forest.

As the forest thickened, the trees of the outer forest were replaced by enormous trees that dwarfed those that came before them. They towered at heights even greater than the broken remains of the tallest buildings of Phoenix. The leaves, most more than twice the size of her hand, cast so many shades of green that it reminded her of a polished alien gem she had seen on the space station. It had swirled with so many hues that it was entrancing, even as its cut made it sparkle with life. That gem could almost have been the perfect recreation of the hues of the forest she now walked through. Even the fine hairs that covered the leaves of many of the trees, and the thick dusting of silver hairs on vines, made the forest sparkle in the sunlight.

There was another vine that came from the tree covered with a dusting of dark, jewel-tone red hairs. The protrusions that grew out from the sides of the trees swayed in the air, not unlike Veral's vibrissae. Terri couldn't see any reason for them to have them—not until she watched one catch a large insect and drag it into a hole just above it. Their constant movement unnerved her, especially whenever she caught a sharp movement from one of the vines out of the corner of her eye. It made Terri tense with anxiety, fearing that another animal was preparing to pounce.

After all, there was plenty of cover to conceal any number of creatures. Clinging to the sides of the trees and filling in the gaps between them were fronds, bushes, and vines, and so many types of flowers in hues of reds, pinks, blues, pink, and even silver in tiny sprays, large blooms and thick clusters that it was magical.

A magical place where anything could hide. Including the drop into the depths of a ravine.

"Halt! Do not move," Veral snarled, his arm banding around Terri so suddenly that her heart almost stopped before she caught a glimpse of what had made him call out to everyone. Shouts went up among the pirates as they drew to a stop and backpedaled with a sense of urgency. Veral's systems, with his ultra-sensitive vibrissae, had picked up something that none of them had seen.

Even Azan drew up short with a sharp gasp of alarm. They had all come too close to their demise.

Terri's heart hammered in her chest above the band of Veral's arm secured tightly around her as she stared down into the chasm of a ravine. Ever since the confrontation with Egbor, her mate had kept her within arm's reach, and she had never been more grateful than she was at that moment. She hadn't even noticed that they were approaching the edge due to the angle at which the trees grew.

It was nothing like what she had expected. She had assumed when looking at the schematic of the crash location with Veral that the forest would open up and the ravine itself would have been nothing but barren rock, not unlike some of the canyons that peppered the landscape where she had grown up.

For one, the trees didn't thin out and part before reaching the sheer stones. Instead, the giant trees seemed to bend and grow at angles as the forest appeared to drop down the walls of the ravine. There was plenty of rock, but if it hadn't been for Veral alerting everyone to the sudden drop, she doubted anyone would have been aware of it.

And it was a long way to fall.

The sound of rushing water from the river below was loud, echoing despite the distance. In a few places, she could see waterfalls cascading down the sheer drops. Terri jerked as a flock of large reptilian birds, disturbed by the presence of outsiders, burst up from a ledge, sunlight bouncing off the vibrant green and red feathers and indigo scales as they winged away, their piercing shrieks reverberating.

"This is unexpected," Egbor muttered as he drew to their side, squinting as he scanned the depths of the ravine. "Are we to go down there?"

"As you are aware, the *Evandra* is farther west. I initially calculated that the only way to approach would be via this ravine.

Whether it is on one of the many ledges or in the water below remains to be seen," Veral replied.

Despite the lack of apparent emotion in his response, Terri knew her mate well enough to know that he was tense and angry, and that the mere presence of the pirate put him in a killing mood. His vibrissae whipped faster, and his mandibles were flexed out in defensive posture.

The captain, however, seemed oblivious—or just didn't care. "This will slow us down considerably. There is no way to arrive at the *Evandra* before nightfall."

"Correct."

"It will not be safe to camp here with our backs to the ravine. We will be at a disadvantage, and vulnerable to anything that hunts us."

"Yes."

Egbor sighed. "What is your suggestion?"

"That we turn around and leave *Evandra* to its rest," Veral rumbled.

The pirate chuckled. "Nice attempt, but that is not happening. Try again. Where would be a safe place to camp that will allow us to arrive at the crash site before nightfall?"

A low hiss escaped her mate as he scanned the cliffs. Finally, Veral jerked his chin, his mandibles clicking, as he gestured to the wide ledge the birds had vacated, some distance away from them. Terri's stomach dropped as she looked at it. Not only would they have to climb down among the trees a considerable way, but traveling along the narrow rocks and outshot trees until they reached the ledge wasn't going to be easy.

The pirate's lips thinned as he noted the location of the ledge. "We go there?" At Veral's short nod, Egbor turned to address his crew. "All of you keep in tight formation. The Argurma has found a suitable ledge for us to make camp on. Make haste. We will not have the sun for long!"

There was some hesitation among the crew, and numerous grumbled complaints as the males noted the location of the ledge and how far they still had to travel before the sun sank below the horizon. Even Azan seemed a bit paler than normal.

"Are you all right?" Terri whispered.

Azan swallowed and her hand tightened around the butt of her blaster, but she jerked her head in a short nod. "I am not a fan of heights, I admit, but I will be fine. That is… quite a drop."

"How the hell is a pirate scared of heights?"

"There are few opportunities to dangle over impossible ledges unless one is stuck somewhere in engineering of a war class fleet ship. Not even the great monstrosity that we crew has any such expanse as that. Fighting in space involves little in the way of heights," Azan replied with the hint of a smile.

"We'll be fine. Just take it slow and we'll make our way over there," Terri said as she swallowed back her own fear. She normally didn't have a fear of heights, but she didn't typically test the whims of fate by walking along ledges with drop-offs that were hundreds of feet deep.

Veral's vibrissae expanded, a soft click rattling from him even while his vibrissae hissed with their own vibrations as he shook his head in the negative. "This ravine is much like the gorge of Ilathitankyu on Argurumal. Best to move quickly. Erosion will make some footholds unstable. The trees and vines will give some added stability, but do not trust that it will remain so. Move as quickly as you can as you pick out your hand and footholds. Stay close to me if you can. I will identify what appears to be the most secure route. I cannot guarantee how long it will hold, but if you are at my side there is a high probability of safe arrival at the ledge."

Azan let out the breath that Terri hadn't even noticed she was holding. The Blaithari circled her head, releasing the tension with tiny cracks and pops.

"I am to trust my life to a male who half a rotation earlier threatened my wellbeing... Very well then," Azan mused with something close to her normal cheer, a crooked smile pulling at the corner of her mouth.

Veral narrowed his eyes on the pirate and made a sound like a dismissive growl mixed with a laugh before turning away to address the more immediate problem: the climb down.

Terri wrapped her fingers around the horn protruding from his elbow, clinging to him, though his arm didn't move away from her as he angled them at the edge of the chasm. Glancing down, his glowing blue gaze met hers and he squeezed her, trying to comfort her.

"You will do well," he assured her. "Remember the training."

"Of course," she agreed and took a deep, steadying breath.

This was part of the game of being a salvager. In space, she prepared for months for situations such as this. This trip would prove what she learned. The pirates were an unanticipated addition, but having to climb from great heights was something that she did over and over again in the simulations, in addition to the physical training Veral had her do in the cargo bay on the obstacles he had constructed.

It was just climbing. She had this.

Still, she couldn't hold back the tiny squeak of distress that left her when Veral released her and stepped away. His eyes pinned on her, his vibrissae stirring with their vibrations as he peered down at her.

"Close behind," he reminded her.

He didn't move until she nodded and followed him to the ledge. Immediately, Veral gripped one of the higher branches of a nearby tree and began to drop down its length. The moment he let go of the branch, Terri followed, the weight of her mate's eyes on her as she trailed his path.

She was only vaguely aware of Azan lowering Garswal to the

branch until she heard Egbor's angry shout from above. She tilted her head up and looked beyond the young Blaithari trembling on the branch to the sight of the pirate captain leveling a blaster on his second-in-command. Terri continued to inch toward Veral, but she couldn't look away, her breath caught in her throat at the sudden hostility.

"He is mine, Azan! He will not be going down without me. You are clearly forgetting your place," the captain shouted.

"He will not be able to do anything for you on this climb," his second-in-command retorted.

"I will go next then. By all rights, he is to remain by my side."

"You want him by your side? For what purpose? Never mind, Captain. I yield to your wishes, as always. If you insist on following at his side, I will carry him."

Egbor's mocking laughter could be heard even above the hollow sound of the water and wind growing louder now that they were within the ravine. So could Veral's impatient growl when he turned and noted that Terri wasn't directly behind him. She shot him an apologetic look as she began to move to his side, but half her attention remained on the standoff between Azan and Egbor.

"You wish to be burdened by him? Who am I to object? That he is at my side is all that matters. Just watch your tongue, lest I be tempted to remove it from your mouth. Do not forget that as much churlishness as I tolerate from you, Azan, I will not allow insubordination."

"No insubordination intended, Captain," Azan interjected smoothly. "I am merely unwilling to lose a youngling due to carelessness when it can be avoided." The way the boy had been bitten came to Terri's mind, and she had little doubt that the Blaithari female was also thinking of it as she spoke. "He is not strong enough for this climb alone."

"It would be wise for *someone* to descend," Veral snarled loudly. "Delaying defeats the purpose of staying together."

Egbor let out a bark of laughter, as if amused by Veral's foul temper, and holstered his blaster as he waved Azan forward. The female didn't acknowledge the gesture outside of a tight smile before she gave Veral a half-salute and dropped quickly into the tree.

Whatever fear the pirate had hanging above the ravine, Terri couldn't see a trace of it as Azan climbed quickly over to Garswal and helped him slide onto her back. The boy clung tightly, his tiny claws hooking into her thick vest and his legs wrapping around the female's hips.

"Come, anastha," Veral murmured, the glow of his eyes warm on her.

Terri licked her lips, steeling her nerves, as she slid from the branch she gripped onto another vine-laden tree, her feet scraping against the rocks. Small pebbles broke loose and fell, and small plants tore away. She scrambled when the large stone beneath one of her hands broke free and dropped, the sound of it hitting rocks and branches loud enough to make her freeze until she forced her muscles to keep moving.

The protrusions from the trees that slid over her were distracting, more so when one of them gripped at her hair and tugged slightly before releasing her, but she kept moving over the wall. Her concentration couldn't be spared for anyone other than her mate as she placed her hands and feet in every spot she noted that Veral touched. Keeping his advice in mind, she moved swiftly, putting as little of her weight as possible on her hand and foot holds, until at last she arrived at the side of the ledge.

Veral didn't even wait for her cross onto the wide stretch of rock. His claws dug into the ravine wall as he stretched forward and plucked her from the thick mass of vines she clung to. With one sure movement, he lifted her to the safety of the ledge. The moment her feet cleared, his other arm curled around her until she was wrapped fully in his arms. He didn't set her down, but carried her to the back wall of the ledge, where he dropped down with her held firmly against him.

They sat like that, with Terri sitting between his splayed legs and her back resting on his abdomen and chest, as they watched Azan clear the remaining distance. The female's face was drained of her normal vibrant color, her expression pinched.

Despite how shaky her legs appeared as she landed on the ledge, she didn't crumple with relief or exhaustion. Instead she straightened and walked steadily until she reached their side. Only then did she gently untangle Garswal's death grip from around her. Even after his feet touched the ledge, one of his hands continued to cling to Azan. He didn't even turn to acknowledge Egbor when he dropped heavily to the ledge.

Egbor's strides were almost cocky, his guard trailing behind him like a lost pet, until he stood before them. His eyes immediately fell on Garswal, and he gestured for him to rejoin him. The boy's grip on Azan tightened, his face set in a stony silence as he refused his father's order. Azan stood protectively over him, a small smile on her face.

The message was clear. The boy rejected his father's protection for that of the Blaithari female.

The male's brow furrowed in puzzlement before his expression turned angry. When Garswal still didn't move, the captain shrugged nonchalantly and finally dropped his extended hand as two of his hands fisted at his hips. He proceeded from there to ignore the boy as he looked around, his lips pursing.

"Well done, Argurma, though we could have easily traveled for another hour or more. The sun has not even begun to sink into the horizon. I do not enjoy wasting light."

"The sun drops fast, as you ought to have noticed. The odds that we would find another ledge to rest upon before it became dark are extremely low. Although that would not impede me, it would be reckless for your crew to attempt to climb in the dark.

Without suitable shelter, that is exactly what you would do throughout the night, hoping that you were not plucked off the wall by a predator, or falling to your death from a misplaced hand or foot. If that is an acceptable risk to you, then we can most certainly continue. I would not be able to guarantee the safety of any but my mate, however."

The captain grumbled as he squinted out over the vista. If he wasn't convinced, it didn't appear to bother Veral. Her mate's hand stroked her hair as he held her more firmly against him. The captain's posturing became unimportant as she turned her cheek against his to soak in his warmth and comfort.

"Ah, this must be one of those advantages of mated bliss," Azan mused. "I guess there had to be something—some benefit to tying one's life to a male."

Terri cracked an eye to look at the other female. She would have shot her the finger if the pirate would have had any idea what that meant. Since the effort would have been wasted, she smirked and cuddled farther into Veral's embrace. Egbor's complaints were harder to ignore until a sharp cry and the sound of falling rocks and breaking branches rose over the captain's voice, silencing him. The screams grew fainter as the unfortunate pirate plummeted until he was lost.

"I suppose it is a good plan to rest here," the captain finally conceded.

Azan's derisive snort filled the silence before the crew began milling around to claim a safe place along the ledge. There was a sort of somber sobriety that fell over the males as the stress of losing yet another crewmate began to show.

The tension didn't appear to let up, even in sleep. It was palpable in the air. Everyone seemed to know that the planet had more in store for them, waiting to kill every offworlder who ventured onto its surface. Terri felt it too, and so wasn't surprised when a horrific clatter of numerous shrieking voices descended over the ledge. Terri activated one of the few remaining illumination discs attached to Veral's armor and swallowed back her fear.

From every direction, mouths filled with sharp, needle-like teeth snapped down at them from narrow reptilian heads edged with hard bony beaks at the end of their muzzles. Their long, scaled necks jerked at every effort as enormous claws grappled for purchase. All the while, wide wings filled with glossy feathers beat around them as the animals attempted to pluck prey from among the crew. The disc didn't provide enough light in the open, and they only saw the reptilian birds when they dropped down close. Otherwise, it was just a mass of confusion everywhere in the dark surrounding them.

The strained shouts of pirates filled the night as everyone leaped to their feet, blasters firing blindly into the dark. Only one bird ventured close enough to Terri that, when she brought up her arms defensively, the bio-tech extended a metal band around her wrist from which long barbed whips extended out, snapping at the creature. Although Terri didn't know if any of the blasts landed amid the chaos, she knew that her whips landed, as hot blood splattered on her skin.

Veral's claws were extended, and he slashed out at the creatures whenever they dared to get close. His frustrated snarl at lacking a weapon was all the more obvious when heavy blaster fire from Azan filled the air beside them.

It seemed to last forever, but the assault ended as the birds fled with angry hisses and shrieks. When the last of the calls faded into the distance, the captain rounded on Veral, his face a mask of fury in the glow of the disc.

"*This* is what you call safe?" he shouted.

"When compared to the odds of attempting to travel through the night or camping at the edge of the ravine, it was an acceptable risk. The birds were an inconvenience, and minimal danger."

"How do you figure a minimal danger? They would have killed us all!"

"No one died. The attack lasted only five point three standard minutes, and the lifeforms were relatively easy to frighten away, as I estimated. This is acceptable and normal for salvaging."

The males faced each other, both rigid as they exchanged glares.

"Captain," Egbor's remaining guard called quietly. "I believe that the crew requires your guidance."

"Yes, of course," Egbor muttered as he stalked away, his tone cajoling as he addressed the males. Terri didn't bother to listen to him. She knew it would be appropriately convincing. This was confirmed by Azan's laughter.

"That would be code for 'the crew needs to be talked back into this suicidal mission before everyone revolts,'" Azan said, once the captain was out of earshot.

"Foolishness," Veral growled. He drew a hand down his face. "One more day."

Terri prayed that it wasn't portending something bad coming their way.

20

"It is there," Veral announced as he pointed at a dark shadow deep in the ravine.

Terri clung to a narrow shelf of rock that spanned what must've been a few dozen feet along the wall. Even though everyone hunkered close together, they still all barely fit on it. She swore she could almost feel the rock threatening to crumble beneath her feet as she squinted down in the direction that he indicated.

The starship was as dark as the wreckage that they came upon before, but unlike the medical unit that had been torn away, it was smashed against the rocks in pieces. From the sleek, dark exterior where it wasn't damaged, despite their distance above the remains, Terri could tell that it had once been a magnificent ship. Her eyes scanned over it, greedily drinking it in as everything slipped away. Now confronted with it, she found herself imagining what secrets it might hold.

A small frown pulled at her brow. Although the *Evandra* wasn't completely beneath water, large portions of it were, and that wasn't good. A simulation had predicted such a scenario with a half-sunken vessel. Terri recalled that the exercise had been unpredictable and hazardous. Entering the ship, they wouldn't know what levels were safe and which might be flooded. Due to the pirates' haste, they didn't have the necessary equipment with them to allow for a submerged salvage.

Not that they wanted to help the pirates along, but damn, she wanted whatever was in the ship.

A slight burning sensation drew her attention down to the bio-tech embedded in her forearm, and she grimaced. *Okay, maybe I can live without any more close encounters with the Elshavan.* Still, since they were forced to go down anyway, it would have been nice to be able to walk away with something for their trouble.

"What a glorious sight," Egbor laughed. "Look, all of you, there rests the bounty we have been waiting for!"

"Looks more like a great big invitation into the next world to me," Azan muttered. "It just lacks script announcing 'death awaits you here.'"

The captain nudged his second-in-command with another bark of laughter, blind to the flash of hatred on her face. "Always doom and gloom with you, Azan. This is why you will never be a great captain of your own ship. A captain needs far more pluck."

Azan sneered but kept her face turned away as she spoke in a low voice. "You are right. I would not have captured an Argurma and trapped myself on a planet, dependent on him, for the sake of the promise of a great treasure of which we know nothing about."

"A good captain—a good pirate, even—knows when the risk is worth it," Egbor replied, his eyes narrowing on the female. "Perhaps upon return to the ship I need to weigh whether or not you are the right one to be my second."

"We will drop down to the ship by the vine clusters," Veral began. "You will have to navigate among them to stay on the thicker groupings. Be aware that it will change as you go down, sometimes with gaps between the clusters. Keep to them alone.

The rock here is too sheer for a reliable handhold so there will be nothing to help support your weight elsewhere." Leaning forward, he brushed his lips and mandibles against Terri's jaw. "Move steadily as you have practiced, and your odds of success are ninety-three percent."

She scowled at him playfully. "Only ninety-three? I never fell during simulation."

"No," he agreed with a soft chuff. "But your method of descent has not always been the safest."

"It gets the job done," she whispered as she turned and brushed her lips against his, enjoying the soft scrape of his mandibles at the sides of her jaw. "Don't worry. I'll be right behind you."

Drawing back, Veral clicked his mandibles in approval. Casting one last speculative look at the pirates, his gaze lingering on Egbor as if hoping the male would call off the insanity, he nodded and dropped down onto the first cluster of vines.

Terri watched him as he climbed down quickly until the cluster grew too thin and he promptly swung over to the next cluster at his right. She watched as he repeated this several times without problem. Turning to Azan, she gave the pirate an encouraging smile before she too dropped down to grab the nearest cluster of vines as she slid off the ledge.

Just as she had practiced, she kept her feet braced around the vines as she dropped with a steady hand-under-hand descent. It was different from practicing in the cargo bay or in simulation, but the movement was familiar, and it didn't take her long to begin picking up her pace until she settled into a comfortable rhythm.

Above her, she could hear Azan's muffled curse. The pirate followed her down just as Terri swung over to her second cluster of vines.

Most clusters were within a foot or two of each other, whereas some had a wider spread, but none of them were spaced to a degree that she found challenging. Terri smiled as she navigated among them, steadily dropping closer to the wreckage below.

It was all too easy. So easy that she began to allow herself to slip down the clusters quicker and to skip over those that were closer together as she swung out from one cluster to grab another farther away.

The exhilaration that hit her blood was powerful. She felt like she was flying along the side of the wall as she leaped. She didn't feel weak and helpless, nor at the mercy of the world around her or the cosmos at large. Her lighter body gave her greater mobility than the aliens who were slowly making their way down above her.

From left to right, she worked her way down. Sliding down, her eyes fastened on a long cluster that would close most of the remaining distance of the ravine. It would be a fast descent, dropping her at Veral's side in record time. She just needed to make the jump. It was much further than the previous clusters, but nothing that exceeded what she had been able to manage during training.

She grinned triumphantly at it. She would show herself and everyone that being human wasn't a hindrance or liability. Pulling back on the cluster of vines in her hands, she reversed direction and pushed off, her hand out-stretched for the cluster ahead of her as she leaped.

"*Anastha!*" Veral shouted just as her hand closed around what had appeared to be a suitably thick cluster.

Horror filled her at that very moment she realized that it was nothing more than a single thicker vine with a few thinner vines entangled with it. *It's not a thick cluster!* It wouldn't support her weight. The sound of tearing was incredibly loud to her as the roots ripped away from the wall. Terri instinctively stretched out a hand, her fingernails brushing flat rock. Her breath burst from her in a strangled shout. She had felt fear before, since arriving on the planet, but this consumed her. Everything slowed around her as she fell away from the wall. Veral's bellow of fear even sounded far away.

Azan's words to her so many days ago came back to her, repeating through her mind as she fell. She was too fragile, too vulnerable to survive. Even with the skills she had accumulated, they mocked her as she fell. They weren't enough, and she had been too cocky, so certain of her ability that she hadn't been cautious enough.

Azan was right. Veral, with all his skills and natural ability, had kept her alive ever since he took her away from Earth, and even more recently in the forest. This time, however, Veral was too far away to save her. No one could.

The only one who could save her was herself. Even that would take a miracle. Regardless, she wasn't ready to die, yet.

Tears streaming from her eyes, Terri stretched out her hand, her fingertips too far away to even skim the surface as she dropped back. Growling in frustration, she twisted in the air, and stretched out her hands, willing herself to grab onto something —anything.

She felt it, then.

Something connected as she felt a rush of power through her. The bio-tech burned as hot metal corded over her arm and down her hand, ending in massive metal claws that extended beyond her fingertips. The sound of metal hitting rock squealed in her ears, and she reflexively anchored her fingers, curling her new claws into the stone.

Her plummet stopped so suddenly she felt as if her stomach hit her throat, but it was overpowered by a rush of relief. She hung there for a moment, allowing endorphins to flood through her. *I'm alive!*

Terri lifted her head and stared at her hand. The bio-tech had formed an armored glove clear up to her elbow, the green center of the symbiont pulsing with energy. She had activated it. Twice now, she had managed to activate it when overcome by a powerful desire. There was a key somewhere in that. A way to connect to the bio-tech and utilize it.

"Anastha... Terri!" Veral shouted up, relief unmistakable in his voice, as was the bite of anger.

"Yeah, I'm coming down!" she shouted back.

Intently ignoring the sound of Azan's breathless laughter, Terri lightly swung herself until her other hand curled around another cluster of vines. That particular cluster had some terrible smelling plant twined within it, but she wasn't in any position to complain. Instead, she tried to view it as a sort of penance as she made her way down until she reached a point where she could transfer to another vine.

Twice more, she repeated the process until she dropped down beside Azan, the black metal beneath her feet surprisingly silent with the exception of a light, muffled thump. The female wrapped an arm around her and squeezed briefly in a tight hug before letting her loose.

"You may be a little, soft thing, but you are certainly crazy," the Blaithari female chortled. "It scared a half-dozen revolutions off my life. I cannot believe you made it," she pronounced with a grin, her eyes gleaming as they settled on the clawed glove.

Terri flexed her hand self-consciously as she grinned back at Azan. The smile, however, turned sheepish as she met Veral's regard. Immediately, her skin cooled as the bio-tech disengaged and uncoiled from her arm, leaving her bare and exposed beneath her mate's glower.

"I know what you're going to say," she said quickly.

A heavy brow lifted speculatively. "I was not aware that telepathy was part of human physiology. But perhaps you are speaking of the numerous times I have instructed you during training to take the predictable and logical route. To not overextend for no other reason than that you can."

"You are angry, aren't you?"

"Furious," he growled. "We will address this matter with considerably more training... repeatedly, once we are finished here. The simulation on scaling down foreign walls and vertical surfaces until I am satisfied will suffice."

Terri frowned at the thought of hours and hours scaling the cliffs of Abzorra Thranal, Veral's favorite training programing. One he had drilled her in for weeks until he felt satisfied, despite his displeasure with her antics. Just that quickly, his anger dissipated, and he drew her against him, nestling her within his embrace.

"I am very pleased, however, that you have come back to me safe, anastha," he whispered against her hair.

A low purr rumbled around her from his vibrating mandibles, and she instinctively melted against him. Her endorphin rush finally bottomed out as she sagged against him, a tremble working through her muscles as he held her close. She was distantly aware of the sounds of feet hitting metal as the rest of the pirates joined them, but she pushed it away, relishing her moment with him.

Unfortunately, the captain wasn't the patient sort who took well to being ignored.

"Enough with the loving reunion. Your mate is safe, and the crew is all here with the *Evandra* herself beneath our feet. No more delays," Egbor snapped impatiently.

As Terri pulled back from Veral's arms, she noted that the captain had a feverish light to his eyes as he stared down at the dark hull of the starship. His pupils were blown wide as his gaze twitched with a sort of frantic restlessness that could only be obsession.

She lusted over whatever the ship held as well, but that half-mad look on his face made her draw deeper into Veral's embrace, reluctant now to set foot inside. She didn't even want to touch the thing, and would have crawled up onto her mate if there wasn't a risk of making herself appear even more foolish than she had already managed.

Whatever dwelled within there couldn't be worth that.

Her opinion didn't change when Veral led them to where his scans indicated the entrance hatch was located. It opened with little effort from him, seeming to respond to him in a similar manner to how the medical unit had. This time, however, the ship didn't power down when he disconnected from the door. Instead, the interior lit up.

A voice echoed from the ship's interior. It took her translator a moment to catch up since she hadn't studied the Elshavan texts as much as Veral. She sucked in a breath when the words finally sorted themselves out in her mind.

"Welcome, Captain."

21

"*Captain*? This salvager is not captain. I am the only captain here," Egbor bellowed, his head craning around as he addressed the *Evandra's* AI.

"Negative," the cool voice responded. "Scans indicate that you do not have starship interface implants required of those with captain-level clearance. There is only one being present with such implants who has initiated uplink with the *Evandra*."

Egbor turned on Veral with a savage expression. "Keeping secrets from me, were you Argurma?"

"Not secrets for those who know anything about the Argurma species. That you are ignorant of our implants for tech interface is no fault of mine," Veral replied.

The pirate's face darkened with anger and embarrassment. Veral kept his amusement to himself, but took pleasure in seeing Egbor rattled. The captain had been upstaged by a salvager, and he did not like it. Veral watched the male, calculating the odds of an attack. Despite his anger, the odds were low. Egbor didn't get where he was by merely reacting. He was too smart for it.

Just as Veral predicted, an easy smile replaced the captain's scowl, though the tension lingered around his eyes, despite his forced joviality. He cut a quick glance toward his crew, weighing their reaction. The pirates were watching the interaction far too closely.

"Not that it matters," Egbor said quickly. "Communication with the ship's AI is a boon to our cause regardless of who accomplishes it. The starship doesn't know any better when it comes to who really holds the power, and as long as we can gather information from it, it will serve our purpose." He relaxed further and gestured with a wide sweep of his hand. "Go ahead, *Captain*, find out where our treasure is."

A sneer of distaste pulled at Veral's lips. Predictable. Although his mate had a lust for wealth, it was merely to satisfy her needs. The fact that credits ensured that she ate and had comforts was the only use she had for it. For the captain, it was a different matter. The pirate's greed lit up his eyes with a fever, making them overly bright, willing to risk all for his treasure.

"Are you certain? It is not too late to turn back. This ship should not have been disturbed. No treasure is worth that."

"The treasure is worth everything and more," the male hissed, and Veral nodded.

It was exactly as he had calculated.

His arm tightened around Terri as he addressed the *Evandra*.

"Locate any wealth stored on the *Evandra*."

"There is a storage room that belonged to the younger prince, Nahsalva. His valuable possessions were kept under lock there off his main chambers. My systems indicate that you do not have clearance to open the royal compartments, and the accessway is flooded."

Egbor's eyes lit up. "We will find a way into them. Acquire the directions to the royal compartments, Argurma. Do not forget the reason we are here, and our particular arrangement."

Veral did not need a reminder. Clutching his mate protectively to him, he glared at the male as he spoke to the AI.

"*Evandra*, are there any lifeforms residing around the compartments?"

A length paused followed as a diagnostic ran, the pattern of the corridors and rooms scanned flowed as script behind his eyes.

"Negative, captain. There are no detected local life forms within the *Evandra*."

"Rephrase, are there any bio-tech classified experiments operating around the compartments or anywhere within the ship?"

"Affirmative. Two classified bio-tech lifeforms have been detected. One has established hunting territory in the vicinity of the lower deck laboratory units. The other is in the flooded upper deck compartments. These are the only ones with established territory on the *Evandra*. The other thirteen lifeforms escaped onto the planet. Wide range scans indicate that they have migrated a considerable distance from their point of origin."

"We will need directions," Egbor pressed, and Veral barely contained his desire to rip the demanding male's head off, if for no other reason than to shut him up.

"Kaylar, your expedient arrival would be appreciated."

"Understood. I am descending now, preparing to enter the planet's stratosphere. I have homed in on your location. Unlike your unwieldy salvager, I am in a war-class drop ship. I will arrive at your position in just a few hours. Be sure to leave some carnage for me."

"It will be my pleasure, cousin," Veral returned.

"*Evandra*," he said aloud, "upload pertinent schematics and bio-tech signatures into the uplink."

"Affirmative, captain," the AI replied.

It was the only warning he got before the information surged into his systems. With it, he was able to feel the ship as a part of himself as he became intimately aware of every inch of the vessel. He could even feel the movement of the bio-tech creatures as they prowled through the bowels of the starship. There was so much that he could feel the strain on his systems, his muscles tightening and his throat raw as a roar ripped from him with the unyielding pressure. Through the pain, he focused on the soft touch of his mate's hand and the warmth that flowed from her, anchoring him until the transfer completed.

"Well?" Egbor demanded.

A clicking growl rattled from Veral's chest as he glared at the pirate. "I have it. We may proceed."

Keeping Terri close at his side, Veral made his way into the ship, the lights flickering on in each section of the corridor at their approach. Although he was aware of the crew following them, it was only by listening intently that he was able to distinguish their individual steps on the metal walkway of the ship.

This part of the vessel, at least, was not tipped to the side or upside down, which made it convenient to travel upon, but unlike the previous wreckage, broken metal and supplies littered every surface. Among them, fragments of cloth that had yet to decay completely away could be seen. There was no doubt as to what that was, since his scans picked up trace biological material splattered everywhere.

There was only one word for what had happened there: carnage. Absolute, bloody carnage.

The amount of genetic material was so great that Veral stopped, his systems shocked by it. The Argurma had a reputation for the aggression of their warriors, but the bloodbath that had occurred here was so far beyond what was considered acceptable among his people that it was not something he was prepared to see. A skull rolled across the floor, kicked aside by a pirate. Terri stiffened beside him.

"That looks like a skull," she hissed.

"It is."

"That's all you have to say? Is that the only one, or is this entire place just full of shit like that?"

"It may be the only intact skull. This particular corridor, however, has seen the death of dozens, from what I can tell from trace genetic signatures in residue blood spatter and bone fragments scattered over the floor."

"Great…" she muttered. "This is probably going to give me nightmares for years. At least it'll be an incredible story to tell our son or daughter." Her hand smoothed over her stomach as she spoke, filling Veral's heart with warmth with the simple gesture. "That is, if we survive," she muttered, "and don't join the dead here as ghosts ourselves."

"You have an unhealthy obsession with the concept of the spirits of the departed lingering," he observed.

"Says the male who still thinks skulls are romantic gifts," she retorted with an amused smile.

"It is not the skull which is valuable, or the dead who provided it, but the gesture of honoring one's mate by vanquishing all threats to her welfare that has meaning. It means holding one's mate and her honor above all else."

Terri paused, her head tilting to the side as she considered his words. Slowly, her eyes slid over to the captain. "In that case, I look forward to receiving *that* asshole's skull," she whispered as she nodded her head in the captain's direction.

A smile curled his lips as his eyes narrowed on Egbor where he trailed near Veral's side. It would be a great pleasure to do just that.

22

Once she knew what to look for, Terri couldn't unsee the destruction and needless death everywhere. The experiments had ravaged the crew, killing everyone trapped in the starship with them. She shivered as she tried not to imagine the screams, and yet they seemed to surround her, all the same. Veral didn't believe in ghosts or hauntings, but in her mind, there was little difference between a ghost and the terrible things that her imagination conjured to torment her with.

Her eyes slid over to Egbor, her lips tightening. Ever since entering the ship, he no longer lingered behind them, staying on Veral's left with his guard tagging close beside him. There was an eagerness about him, as if he were waiting to be the first to set upon whatever he could find.

Part of her wondered if he was posturing for the crew, and that was possibly some small part of it, but on the whole he was motivated by his desire to possess the wealth of the *Evandra* at any cost. She almost felt sorry for the Blaithari male standing guard at the captain's side as they made their way deep into the starship.

There seemed to be a certain weight that surrounded them—a stench of death—and a tangible presence of the unknown that she felt the farther they went into the ship. It made her skin prickle and a shiver crawl up her spine.

Azan's muttered chants under her breath did little to calm Terri's anxiety as they made every step feel like venturing into a forbidden place. She wanted to shout and beg the other female to be silent—anything to reduce the ominous feeling that accompanied them into the depths of the starship.

Every now and then, she swore she felt a tremor echo through the ship. Although no one said anything, she knew that Veral noticed it from the way he tensed, and the wary shift of his gaze as he attempted to pinpoint the origin, his vibrissae vibrating as he searched for any hint of the creature moving through the ship. Even the pirates appeared to still, their eyes roving nervously.

Despite the rumbling echoes that trembled throughout the ship, they moved without any sign that they were nearing the abode of any of the bio-tech creatures. Terri could almost pretend that the monsters weren't lurking within the starship.

That illusion disintegrated the moment the door to the upper deck slid open at Veral's approach, releasing the stale air and stench of rot captured within out into the corridor. Terri gagged at the horrible smell, her stomach churning as they stepped inside. They hadn't taken more than a few steps when the AI's voice echoed around them.

"Warning. You have entered the upper deck habitation zone. There is a water breach on the forward quarters. Immediate evacuation is recommended. Repeat, immediate evacuation is recommended."

"Immediate evacuation for a bit of water, never mind the murderous bio-tech swimming around somewhere down there," Terri mumbled as she peered around nervously.

For a habitation zone, the corridor was just as dark and featureless as any other part of the ship she had seen. The only thing that broke the seemingly endless depths were the doors that lined each side of the hall, their angle emphasizing the fact that the floor sloped at a hard tilt. Some opened at their passing, revealing empty rooms, but most remained shut, likely occupied by the remains of their inhabitants who had attempted to hide from the creatures, only to die horrible deaths in the crash.

One door that opened confirmed that possibility as her eyes fell on the remains of an Elshavan against a wall. Whoever the poor bastard had been, they had clearly died in their attempt to take refuge in the empty room. They escaped the monster, but it hadn't made their fate any better.

A heaviness curled deep within her at the clear evidence of the sad fate of the Elshavan as they silently walked down the hall. As terrible as it was to see the signs of massacre throughout the halls of the ship, the sight of the Elshavan dying without any way of escape made the dread sink deeper into her.

No one had escaped the *Evandra* alive.

Hopelessness filled the vile air, and alarm raced through her when a little splash rose with her every step. They had finally descended far enough into the zone that they were entering the flooded part of the starship. Her lips pressed together, thinning anxiously as the water began to climb until it covered her foot, and then rose above her ankle.

Just how deep was the water in the flooded part of the ship? Despite how disconcerting it was, she took some comfort from the fact that Veral wasn't concerned. A soft growl was the only indication of his displeasure as the water climbed. Even those who survived among the crew had fallen silent as they endured the biting cold of the water as it came waist-deep on Terri. It was considerably shallower for most of them since only the amphibious Turogo were the height of humans.

"How much farther is it?" Egbor asked, his nose wrinkling in distaste as the murky water soaked the finely embroidered cloth of his long overcoat.

"At the end of the corridor," Veral replied. "The *Evandra's* scans show that the area is not completely flooded, but the water will get deeper still." He glanced meaningfully to Azan. "The youngling may need to be carried…"

She gave him a sharp nod and turned, gripping the boy as she swung him effortlessly onto her back once more. She grinned. "He'll be my personal parasite passenger until we get out of this accursed death pit, on my honor."

"I am not a parasite," Garswal grumbled but smiled as he tucked his chin beside the female's neck.

Egbor made a disgusted sound in the back of his throat. "Bah, keep him! No doubt a female such as yourself will never spawn any young, given that I never managed to get a proper heir off you. Useless female. Might as well mother a useless half-breed male," he sneered. "You deserve the parasite, as you so aptly call him."

Terri watched as Azan's smile dropped away, her expression turning cold and hard. She wondered if the female would attack then. Every muscle coiled with tension, just waiting to spring upon the male.

Egbor laughed and opened his arms. "If you wish to attack, then do so, Azan. I will see to it that you are put down like a crazed beast for your mutiny."

The entire crew stilled, their attention riveted to the pair. Azan's eyes flicked over to them, and she noticeably relaxed, the tension draining away as if it had never been there, an easy smile spreading across her face.

"It does not appear that doing so would be in my best interest, *Captain*," she said with a twist of her lips as she adjusted Garswal's weight. "I hate you with all the fire of two suns, but I am yours, as always."

The captain chuckled, the sound out of place in the empty silence of the tomb that the *Evandra* had become. "And that is why you are my second. You hate me, yes. I see it in your eyes just as I saw it every time that I laid with you, but you are my weapon. You know no other existence than your service to me. I know you too well, Azan. You will never risk everything."

Terri wasn't so sure about that. She would already have killed the captain herself if she had access to any kind of reliable weapon, and if the threat of the pirate ship didn't hang over them. Azan's position was different, but no less delicate if she had any plan to exact the vengeance that Terri had seen brewing within the female without serious repercussions.

Her eyes trailed over to the remaining Igwins. There hadn't been many to begin with among the crew, and the captain had brought every one of them, as if they were his personal hounds. Now there were only five left, but even at their reduced number, they still made her uncomfortable. Hell, one alone would be enough to do the job. She couldn't help but stare as they moved with an anxiety she had never seen in the predators.

Their full attention had been focused just moments earlier on Azan, not with the sexual hunger that Terri often felt focused on her, but with a certain amount of fear that made her wonder what Azan had done to inspire it. Now, however, they were eyeing the water ahead. The nostrils in their muzzles flared, and their large eyes rolled, betraying their nerves.

One turned his head to look back at her, his orange tongue slipping out hungrily as he licked his teeth. It didn't last long, however, before he was once more staring out at the water further down the corridor. Regardless of what his instincts demanded of him, his fear was far more powerful.

Terri squinted as she peered down the hall, her heart leaping as she saw what appeared to be a large fin push out from the water. A very, *very* large fin. It sank down and disappeared so quickly that it almost appeared to be a trick of shadows, but she knew what she saw.

"Veral…" she whispered as she reached forward and grabbed his arm.

"I am aware," he murmured, his blue eyes scanning the water. His hand closed around hers as he cautiously led her forward, farther down the hall. "Stay close, anastha. It seems to have withdrawn for the moment, likely to draw us deeper into the water where it can efficiently kill us, but it will return."

"What is it?"

"Ship systems appear to identify it as Experiment 226. An aquatic destroyer. Large tubular body covered with fins for accurate fine motor abilities in addition to a large dorsal fin and tail. It escaped from its containment tank when the hull was breached in the western laboratory unit and followed the river until it made its home in this sector of the ship. It hunts by echolocation in the water, releasing vibrational songs once every hour, though the frequency increases to once every six standard minutes when it enters frenzy mode. Its range is impressive, but we have not yet approached close enough for it to notice our presence."

"Fuck. Will we be able to get into the storage area before it returns?" she asked.

"Unknown. The odds are difficult to calculate. There are too many unknown variables regarding fallen structures farther within the ship that may reduce mobility in parts of its territory, or whether wildlife will travel within the vicinity of its den to lure it out into the river."

"Why would it attack wildlife?"

Veral slanted her a surprised look. "Because it still has biological needs. It requires an energy source. It is why the Elshavan made the weapons as hunting beasts. It was so that they could acquire energy from natural feeding processes. It cannot reproduce, but so long as it is supplied with energy from feeding, it will continue to exist."

"What is that?" Azan called out, her arm shaking as it rose to point to what looked like a partially sunken metallic skeletal frame.

It was horrific. Terri couldn't imagine what it must have looked like alive. Although the skeleton lay at an odd angle that made it difficult to discern specific features, she was able to note what looked like a long, barbed tail that appeared to stretch out behind it at. What was far more noticeable was its long, narrow skull. With four huge orbital sockets, it no doubt had keen sight, but more disturbing were the massive tusks that jutted up from its jaw, surrounded by two rows of sharp teeth, each surpassing the length of her arm. Massive claws rested near its head. It was huge, and no doubt had been responsible for much of the mess in the corridor.

"Experiment 195," Veral reported. "Land predator, quadruped with camouflage capabilities. It had a reinforced musculature and aerodynamic frame that would have allowed it to run at high speeds. It appeared to have been caught in this part of the ship during the crash. With the flooding, the emergency closure of the area would have made it impossible to escape. Without an energy source to hunt, it terminated."

"Terminated, huh? That's the first good news I've had all day," Terri replied.

"I second that," Azan said, a subtle shiver stealing over the pirate as they bypassed it.

She wasn't the only one disturbed by the sight. The crew slowed, lagging behind, their reluctance to continue evident in every step they took. Even Egbor had eyed at it with concern before ordering his guard and a number of his crew to take point in defensive positions around him.

But he didn't call a halt to the insanity.

The dread coiled within Terri sank deeper as they left the remains behind them. The *Evandra* was nothing less than death.

23

Veral was aware of every breath his mate took as the water steadily rose around them. Her eyes were flicking back and forth over the water, tension tightening the muscles of her limbs. There was nothing nearby; he would have sensed it cutting through the water as it approached, but he understood her instinctive need to remain alert. It was wise to be cautious.

The creature hunting within the water was not one to be underestimated. That it was confined to the water made it no less dangerous. Water was unpredictable at the best of times, but that the creature could hide within it and use the hazards of the flooded area against them was concerning.

For that reason, he did not relinquish his grip on his mate as he led the way through the water, following the route on the ship's schematics that would take them to the private quarters of the prince who reigned over the *Evandra*, and the attached storage chamber that contained all of his personal wealth. Veral was confident that he would be able to force access to it. In all the revolutions he spent salvaging, he had never failed to gain access.

That was not what concerned him.

What concerned him was if he would be able to do it fast enough to ensure Terri's safety should Experiment 226 return. Of slightly less concern was how Egbor might react if the treasure he anticipated and promised was not waiting for him. The odds were good that the prince and his wealth escaped the doomed starship before the slaughter reached him.

He compartmentalized these worries, however, devoting his focus to the situation at hand. He knew the moment Terri began to shiver, the armor ineffectual to the prolonged exposure to the cold water as it crept higher. It only just barely reached his chest, whereas the water sloshed above her breasts and occasionally splashed high enough to touch the sides of her neck. Even her hair secured at the back of her head was soaked.

By the time they reached the large door that marked their destination, her teeth were chattering and her lips pale with cold. Despite her low body temperature, she didn't complain as she pushed through the water. Not even the youngling offered any complaint from where he was perched on Azan's back. Silence descended over them like a shadow, the cause easy to identify. Veral was aware of every movement as the pirates looked around nervously with their advance, the sour scent of fear nearly as thick as the quiet.

He tensed as he felt Terri flinch, a startled sound of surprise escaping her, breaking the silence.

"Something touched my fucking leg. Oh, shit—what is that?" she yelped.

Veral's eyes narrowed as he spotted something long moving in the water near her. He identified it just as a shaky laugh left her.

"An alien fish. Thank fuck. It was just a fish."

"Ugly thing," Azan commented, her eyes following it to where it had disappeared beneath fallen debris.

Though Veral refrained from commenting on the observation, he did not understand it. The fish had an enormous rounded head with eyes that took up most of its face with a long, skinny body and narrow tail and fins. It was made to adapt, to thrive in the carved-out riverbed in the ravine. It was perfect for its environment, and this was admirable.

He scanned the area once more for any sign of 226 before turning his attention to the door. Laying a hand on the door, he began to cycle through codes to override the locking mechanism.

"Is this it?" Egbor asked as he pushed closer.

Veral hissed at the male, his snapping vibrissae forcing the pirate to withdraw before he bent his attention once more to the locks. The captain's hand had gone to his blaster, but Egbor settled back to observe without further attempts to speak.

Veral grunted in satisfaction. He could not afford to be distracted.

One glyph settled and locked in place, and then a second. The third eventually locked in as well. He just needed one more and the override would be complete. He felt it then, his vibrissae picking up on the approach of a large object moving in closer. His muscles tensed, readying for attack as he waited for the last glyph to lock.

The water stirred around him, and he heard Terri's breath hitch as she brushed closer, her head whipping around. Slowly, he turned his head and watched a large fin break from the water just as the creature let out a sonic burst. The vibrations washed over him, thrumming through sensors, disorienting his systems. He reeled back, his shoulders hitting the door as he turned his mate in his arms. His body spun to cover her as the final glyph locked in the place.

The door slid open, water flooding into the once sealed room. Thrusting Terri away from him upon entering, Veral turned back toward the door, his vibrissae fanning out around him as he braced himself. He was aware of his mate reaching forward to grab Azan's arm, hastening the female through, slowed not only by the drag of water, but by the weight of the youngling on her back. The female would have been swallowed up by the water when Egbor used her body as leverage to push himself through the door if it had not been for Terri's grip on her arm.

The guard did not fare so well.

In an attempt to make his way toward the door, the captain did the same to him, using the male as leverage to shoot forward through the water. Caught off balance by the captain's push toward the cabin, the male's feet came out from beneath him, plunging him into the water. He was only down for a moment before he resurfaced, but when he did, Veral knew the guard would have no opportunity to try to save himself.

Screams broke out as the male was pulled beneath the waves, disappearing once more. Terror filled the male's face seconds before he vanished again beneath the surface. This time, however, he did not emerge.

He was followed by another, but that male's cries were drowned out by the panicked shouts of the pirates as they rushed to the door, their limbs thrashing in their desperation to flee from the corridor.

Pitilessly, Veral commanded the door to shut.

The door did not slide shut quickly, but fared better than most starships as it pushed through the water. Veral threw his shoulder against it, pushing with all his strength to hasten its progress. Three of the small Turogos managed to swim inside in time, followed by four Blaithari. All else was lost behind the door.

If Veral had been any other male, he might have felt some regret, but he was not. All he felt was a cold satisfaction that those who would have posed a direct threat to him and his mate were gone. For the sake of his female, however, he was glad that the screams were fleeting before silence descended once more. It was only broken by the sharp strikes of 226 as it tested the door. But even that gradually fell into silence.

"Holy shit!"

Terri's soft exclamation drew his attention. Turning away from the door with an agitated whip of his vibrissae, Veral's eyes sought her out and found that she had waded into the room while everyone else had been focused on the door. Even Egbor jerked around in surprise, unaware that the human among them had beaten him to surveying the room.

What the male had been too slow to see was Terri tucking something into a hidden storage compartment on her armor. Instead, he had caught Terri in the act of scooping up a small pile of gems arranged on a table beside the high bed on which she sat. Just behind her, Veral could make out what was left of the prince.

A threatening growl rattled from Veral as Egbor strode over to her and leveled his blaster on her. Veral wasted no time moving through the water toward then, his attention locked on the male, tracking his every move.

"Hand them over to me, female," he ordered.

Terri met his eyes, her expression flat as she considered him, her eyes flicking down to the blaster. Shrugging, a smile spread on her face. "Sure thing. Catch!"

The blaster jerked to the side as the pirate lunged for the jewels as she tossed them into the air. The individual plops of them hitting the water were punctuated by the male's cursing as he swept his hand through the water in an attempt to clear the debris enough to see.

"Oopsie!" she sang out, but he was no longer paying attention to her, or to Veral coming up beside him, inserting himself between his mate and the pirate.

"Help me find the jewels!" Egbor snarled to the males clustering at his side.

They pawed frantically through the water, but it did none of them any good. The water merely became murkier as all the washed-in sediment clouded in thick plumes.

As he watched them work, Veral sensed Terri shifting behind him. Her muttered exclamations of disgust as she climbed over the corpse was enough to make him smile despite his fury. That smile widened, his teeth baring when, with a snarled curse, Egbor jerked up, his blaster rising, only for it to be caught in Veral's large hand.

24

Terri watched as Veral leaned in toward the pirate captain. She'd been busy stuffing the sealed storage pouches on her armor. Technically they were made to carry rations and necessary supplies, but since all she had was in the small pack on her back, she decided to put them to better use.

There was plenty to fill them with, that was for sure.

It had been almost amusing to watch the pirates struggle to find a mere handful of jewels in the water. Sure, they were beautiful, but anyone with a sharp eye from years of scavenging could've seen there was so much more to be had. The dear prince had certainly surrounded himself with finer things, wealth that would keep their ship stocked and fueled for some time to come.

She thought she had everything under control—distract the pirates with what they want—and snatch up a share for her and Veral for their troubles, but this was unexpected. She had been aware of Veral's large body blocking their view of her, and she had taken advantage of the opening to crawl over his royal deadness, as gross as that had been, in order to pluck up everything of value in sight on the other side of the bed. It seemed that while her attention had been occupied things had certainly escalated.

"That is the last time you will threaten my mate," Veral snarled, each word punctuated by the deadly hissing rattle of his vibrissae.

He didn't even appear to notice that the other seven pirates had drawn their weapons and aimed them at him. Or if he did, he wasn't worried about them. She knew that Argurma were hard to kill, but even she was concerned about her mate taking that many direct shots from the blasters.

"Males," Azan snorted with disgust, one of her arms wrapped protectively around Garswal. "Take note of this behavior," she said to him. "It rarely accomplishes anything. It is far better to keep a calm, collected mindset than to be so reactionary. Right now, cooperation serves our purposes far better. That is the route to go—until it does not."

"Cooperation," Egbor agreed with a smirk. "Or the death of you and your mate. Perhaps drawing my weapon was a small overreaction, but I am a pirate. Threatening is part of the job description, especially when my blood is up. I would not have harmed her while she still served some use. In that way, Azan is correct."

Veral tilted his head as if he were listening. The lethal smile widened before it fell away. "Cooperation," he snarled. "Very well. We shall... *cooperate*."

Very slowly, he released the blaster, and as his hand pulled away Terri could see the bent metal. He had crushed it, rendering it useless. The captain's face reddened when he saw it, but he schooled his expression into a tight smile. Veral inclined his head and withdrew, his eyes never once leaving Egbor.

Without a word, he strode toward a door at the side of the room, the water sloshing at his hips. His eyes slid over to her, and he gave her a tiny, almost imperceptible shake of his head, a movement that would have been difficult for most to catch among his writhing, vibrating vibrissae.

He didn't want her to follow him.

Terri darted a look over at Azan, but the pirate remained at the far corner with Garswal, her face almost relaxed as she watched the eager greed rise in Egbor as he hurried after Veral.

"No tricks this time!" the captain called out as he struggled to catch up to the Argurma's greater speed and longer stride as they pushed through the water. "I will be first through this time. I will not tolerate any more loss of wealth from mischievous females and their games."

Terri smiled innocently and lifted her hands in front of her in the universal gesture of surrender. "I won't even dream of coming in," she said agreeably.

There was enough for her to continue to lift from the room she was already in.

She didn't need to enter the treasury, though she had to admit that she was curious to see it. Pirates' gold was a thing of dreams and fairytales. To be that close to it… No. Veral didn't want her to enter. Egbor eyed her suspiciously, but she sat on the bed once more and patted the embroidered cloth covering one of the prince's skeletal arms. "Princey and I will keep each other company until you return."

Egbor grunted and nodded at the remains. "Be of some use then and strip that robe. Those fibers are of a quality to last for generations, according to rumor, and it appears the rumor is true. I want that robe for myself. It will be the finest thing in my wardrobe."

Terri balked, her hand dropping away. "You want me to remove it from a dead body? So you can wear it?"

That's sick.

Apparently he was determined, because his eyes did not move from her until she reluctantly turned and began to pull the sleeve from the corpse. The bones fell out from the sleeve, along with the dust of decay. She swallowed back her bile and yanked the robe out from beneath the skeleton, the bones rolling from it, scattering over the bed. Gray matter dusted the forearms of her armor. Gingerly, with one hand, she plucked off a few smaller bones that were stubbornly clinging to the fabric.

"This is so disgusting," she mumbled as she yanked the other arm out of the robe, freeing it of bones and plucking off the few remaining strays before rolling the fabric up. She held it out, certain she was going to throw up at any moment.

Scurrying over the body was one thing. Direct contact made her stomach turn.

"Your robe, Captain."

A smug smile curled his lips, no doubt noticing how green the entire situation was making her. "Put it into your pack and carry it for me. I will need mine to fill with treasure. I will recover it from you once we return to the ship."

Terri grimaced and swung her pack from her back. "Sure. Just... awesome."

She tried not to think about the nastiness that it would be getting all over everything as she shoved the rolled-up material into her bag. As far as she was concerned, anything within it was now tainted from the contact, including the food rations and hydration pods that were divvied up the last time they stopped out of concern over having the food all with one individual, with the way the crew was dying off. In light of how few people survived the encounter with Experiment 226, as Veral called it, she'd been grateful. Now that they were buried in the crumbly remains of a dead prince... well, she was no longer hungry. She hoped that Veral had been given some rations to carry.

She shouldered the bag again and looked back toward the pirates, noticing that they were no longer paying attention to her. His orders being followed, Egbor had resumed focus on his objective: getting into the room. He drew up to Veral's side, his face tight with expectation as Veral worked on the door codes.

The door unlocked and slid open as Veral stepped back to permit the captain entrance. Egbor didn't even hesitate, pushing his way through, a joyous shout coming from him. Terri's eyes widened at what she could see from where she sat.

There were visible containers of gold, precious metals she couldn't even identify from the distance, and gems that put the palm-sized ones she had ferreted away to shame. Most containers were large enough that they stood above the water level like brilliant beacons, but even those beneath it glittered beneath the artificial lighting that had activated when Veral opened the door. In fact, the water seemed to lend mystery to those it concealed, and Terri had to wonder what was hidden on the floor, obscured by the sediment.

She blinked. *Wait... Water?*

The prince's chamber hadn't been flooded until they opened it. Why was the treasure room already flooded? It appeared to have been for some time, the lower ends of several tapestries rotting and falling apart where they were submerged. That didn't make sense, unless...

Egbor laughed, his arms stretched out as he circled. "Is it not as I told you!? Behold the wealth of the *Evandra*! It is ours!"

Hands dove among the treasures, eagerly filling packs to the brim as Veral took one step back and then another to place his hand once more on the key panel. Terri sucked in a breath as he initiated the sequence to seal the door once more. The pirates spun around just as the door began to slide shut, panic on their faces, but what Terri saw made her blood run cold.

An enormous fin broke free of the water, and a deafening shriek filled the room.

They shouted in fear, scrambling for the door. Veral grinned ruthlessly at Egbor, who had waded too far into the room to make it back in time. The captain shouted as he made his way to the door, only then noting the creature emerging behind them.

"*Wait!* Argurma, you cannot leave us in here!" he bellowed.

"I told you, did I not, that you would never threaten my mate again?" Veral said just as the door slid home, the heavy chink of the locking mechanism engaging filling the room. He turned away from the door just as the screaming began and looked at Azan.

"Will I have any trouble from you, pirate?"

A lazy smile stretched over the female's face, and she shook her head. "From me? Not at all. With no Igwins left on the ship, I will be able to exact complete control and put things back in shape that his endless greed allowed to fall apart. In fact, I would say that this may put me in your debt for ridding me and the crew of that overbearing male."

Terri sloshed over to his side, a tremor running through her when the last hair-raising scream split the air. "That might set some kind of record for vengeance delivered. Send the guy to be eaten by a monster. Well done."

He smirked down at her, his vibrissae smoothing through her hair. "It would be lauded among my people, though I lost the trophy," he said, his smile falling.

"I'd say it was worth it. Something worthy of legends, far better than a skull." A puzzled frown pulled at her brow. "But how are we going to get off the planet? The pirates…" She cast a hopeful look to Azan, but the female shook her head.

"Although I fully intend to take over the crew, it will not be so easy as that. I will need to return to the ship and wrest control. That takes time—and a lot of blood spilled, if I'm unlucky. I do hate to lose crew members, but I will have to deal with those who consider themselves loyal to Egbor. We still need to devise a way off this planet, and to return us to the ship, without being blown out of the sky. By now, his vitals implant will have flatlined. His upper crew will be aware of his death. They will have been alerted by medical immediately."

"Fuck! What are we going to do?"

"Do not be concerned. I have a contingency plan en route," Veral replied.

"What?" Terri asked, bewildered.

"We will no doubt have to deal with him as well, but it will allow us to get away from the pirates." Veral tilted his head again, smirking. "He is arriving now. We must leave."

"Let's hope we don't meet up with 226 on our way out," Terri muttered. "How did you know it was in there?"

"My scans revealed that the room was flooded and a large bio-organic tech was present. It was clear that the thing had made the treasure room its den. I estimate that we will be able to pass through the flooded compartments before it realizes that there is more prey awaiting it."

"Please don't refer to us as prey," Terri groaned.

"Yes, please," Azan muttered as she swung Garswal onto her back. "Lead the way, then."

25

Veral noted the longing look that Terri gave the room, no doubt wishing to scavenge for anything that captured her attention. If this had been a normal salvage job, he would have been pleased to watch the joy on her face.

"We do not have time to linger," he said quietly at her side, his hand grazing her arm as he gently nudged her forward. It was perhaps unnecessary, but still it required saying for clarity sake. "I am sorry that I cannot give you more."

A small sigh escaped from her, but she met his eyes and nodded. "I know. None of that went down the way it should have, but we have what's most important. We're both alive."

"Let us not celebrate prematurely," Azan interrupted dryly as she headed toward the doorway. "We have not escaped yet."

There was nothing to say following that. Although they had survived to that point, events could follow which would tip fortune out of their favor. For that reason, instead of speaking further, Veral stepped out into the hall. He froze, his vibrissae whipping and vibrating around him as he stretched his senses to pick up any trace of 226 approaching. He could sense the smaller life forms in the water around them, but thankfully the creature was absent.

Half-turning, he gestured for his mate to follow him out. She hurried out of the royal cabin back into the corridor, the water rippling all around her as she rushed through it. Veral tensed, certain that the vibrations from the moving water would alert the creature. He still could not detect any sign of movement from it, but that did not mean it was unaware. Azan splashed after her, causing more disturbance. His muscles tightened, but he forced himself to temper the reaction, even as his systems went on high alert, increasing his surveillance of their surroundings.

The moment she joined them, he struck out ahead, half of his attention remaining on Terri to make sure she was not struggling to keep up as he plowed ahead to where the water broke. Terri stumbled at his side, ragged gasps for air escaping her as she labored to maintain his pace.

The water dragged at them, her worst of all, but gradually the waterline dropped, making their movement easier and faster. The dark floors rising from the water drew closer with their every effort to surge forward. His body tightened, triumph filling his blood with liquid fire as they drew closer.

They were close to dry ground when he felt it.

Veral stopped, the water splashing around him in broken crests as he turned to look back even as he pushed Terri forward. His mandibles clicked softly, a thoughtful sound just as he watched the monstrous fin break free from the water. The hunt had begun!

Hissing, he whipped back around and leaped forward, driving his body through the water with all of his strength. Reaching out, his fingers closed around Terri's upper arm, dragging her with him. Azan's startled exclamation rang out behind him as she too took note of the creature advancing on them. Panting breaths filled the air amid the dragging, splashing sounds all around them. Even the splashing, however, could not dull the ripples he felt race toward him, punctuated by the sonar shriek of the creature attempting to precisely locate them.

Spurred on by its rapid approach, Veral grabbed one of Azan's muscled arms and yanked her forward with him as well. Together they raced as the creature barreled after them, water breaking around its girth as it began to surface.

A large wave rolled forward, knocking them all off their feet at the exact moment the creature's girth rose through the water. Veral's fingers curved, his claws extending to dig into the ship's floor as he pulled himself forward, gaining his footing again. Azan sputtered but rose to her feet quickly as she pulled Garswal from the water, the young male coughing out fluid as he hunkered against her, his wet hair streaming rivulets all around him and over Azan's shoulders. Terri choked, coughing as she rose from beneath the surface, but she stumbled forward determinedly. Veral grabbed her arm as she reached for him. A growl rose in his throat as they pushed forward again.

"Do not look back. Just run," he commanded as he saw her turn her head.

"Oh, fuck—too late. *Too late!* I saw it! Oh my gods!" she cried out.

"Not looking!" Azan shouted as she surged forward, her legs kicking up higher as she made every attempt to increase her speed in the now thigh-deep water. "If Egbor was not already in the belly of that thing, I would kill him for this alone!"

Terri's breath came out in rapid pants as she attempted to run faster. The water rippled around them violently as 226 raced toward them, its shrieks rippling and echoing through the cavernous corridor.

With a snarl, Veral turned and grabbed his mate around the hips, lifting her from the water as he vaulted her over it. Her scream was cut short with a loud breath as she hit the dry ground. Turning, he grabbed Azan next and ignored her snarl as he repeated the move, hurling her and Garswal as far as he could. The female pulled the male into her arms and curled around him midair. When they landed with a splash in the shallow water close to where Terri lay on the dry floor, the pirate had absorbed the full impact.

The water quaked everywhere, droplets bouncing from the surface at its approach. He was not going to be able to outrun it. His eyes fell on his mate as she pushed to her feet. Her hand cradled her ribs as she grimaced, but her expression turned to one of terror.

"*Veral!*" she screamed, grief trembling in her voice.

It was too late. He turned, slashing out with his claws, his vibrissae whipping out in defiance just as the large maw of the predator opened wide, a crest of water rushing over him. Metallic teeth descended just as a large metallic barb struck it. Veral felt a piercing pain scream through him. It was echoed by the terrible screams of pain from the creature as it thrashed behind him.

Despite the red-hot pain and alarm flashing through his systems, he turned away from the thing, racing forward again. The barb, possessing the same bio-organic signature of the symbiont, had bought him time. Azan grabbed him at the same time Terri did, both females helping to haul him to dry ground as he stumbled forward. Tattered remains of several vibrissae on the right side of his head attempted to writhe in their instinctive need for input, sending shooting pain through him.

He could already feel his nanos rushing to the spot in an attempt to heal it. It would take time, but they would mend. Until then, he felt off balance, the sudden loss of a part of his sensory receptors making him move with uncertainty, a large blind spot now at his right.

An Argurma with injured vibrissae was vulnerable. This was a hazardous place to be vulnerable, especially with his mate in danger.

She and his unborn offspring needed him.

Turning back, he glared at 226. Its body writhed and splashed, terrible shrieks still coming from it as it rolled in the shallow water. It was pushing away from them, flopping to push its girth back into deeper water. From one of its lower eyes, he could see the barb jutting out, dark blood spurting from the wound. Eventually, it would heal. It was not a killing shot any more than its bite, its aim disrupted, was a killing strike to Veral.

They were both left with injuries from their encounter, but they both would survive.

"Veral, thank the gods," Terri whispered, her hands running over him in self-assurance. Her hand raised to the side of his head and she winced. "Your vibrissae…"

"Their loss is better than dead, or any greater damage. I will heal," he murmured as he pulled her hand down and brought it to his lips. "You are safe. That is what is most important to me."

She gently pulled her hand back and punched his shoulder. "Damn it, Veral! Stopping to throw us out of the water slowed you down. You nearly got yourself killed. You shouldn't have done that. We could have made it!"

"Speak for yourself," Azan muttered, two pairs of her arms wrapped around Garswal, comforting the young male who had finally broken down and curled against her with soft sobs. "I, for one, am grateful. Not only for my life, but for his as well." The pirate glanced over at Veral, her expression contemplative. "I do not have much use for males, not even before I was captured by Egbor, and certainly not after revolutions of torture at his hands. But you have made me reconsider that there could be a few males who could be worthy allies and not just crew to follow my orders. I owe you a life debt. If we get out of here and you are ever in need, call on me and I will repay my debt."

The debt of a pirate was one that could be useful if a dire circumstance rose. He eyed her extended hand, the one that had her comm out and activated, the gesture inviting an exchange of comm information. Slowly, he nodded and activated his own comm before reaching out to grip her forearm. It took less than a second for them to exchange details, and even less time for that information to imprint on his systems so he would have it regardless of whether he had his personal comm or not.

He released her hand and stepped away, his attention returning to the bio-tech experiment. He watched it submerge once more until eventually even its fin disappeared from sight.

Turning back to his mate, he regarded her with a new respect. "You have saved my life—again. This repeated theme is disturbing. It seems that your symbiont armor has weapon abilities that I did not consider."

Terri grimaced. "It was luck that it worked at all. Good thing I have good aim. That thing was tiny. Hurt like a bitch, though."

He nodded as his eyes trailed down to the symbiont still glowing on her arm. Terri had pushed the sleeve up to free it. They would have to modify her armor once they were in the ship again. As his was modified for his horns, it would not be difficult. She was already bonding with it and learning how to use it, but they would have to undertake many training sessions and simulations once they were safe to build her control. This symbiont was going to give her safety that he had not imagined she would ever have. He could feel a sense of relief ease someplace that he had not even realized had been wound tight.

His mate would survive, and be in a position to protect their young.

"From what I understand, the symbiont builds from metals in blood and replicates them when it works to protect you, then returns the metals back to your blood when it deactivates. In this case, it released them... I suspect you may feel the side effects from it."

She squinted at him for a moment but nodded reluctantly. "Yeah, I didn't want to mention anything, but I am feeling a bit weak and dizzy. I'm holding onto you not only because I'm happy to see you, but I admit it's also so I don't fall over." She chuckled softly at the pronouncement. "Fucking lot of good I'm going to be helping us to get out of here."

Veral tilted his head. They would have to replicate synthetic boosters for her blood for such situations in the future when she might need them. *For now, though...* He swept his mate into his arms.

"Veral, put me down, you idiot. You're hurt!"

"I am vulnerable and adapting to the blind spot, yes, but I am still operational. We must leave immediately, and if you are too weak to operate near full capacity, it is logical that I carry you. You will not be able to use the symbiont armor again until you have recovered the loss of metals in your blood."

She grimaced but nodded before settling more comfortably in his arms. "Let's get this show on the road."

He paused. "What show?"

"I don't know. Something my dad used to say. Just means let's get moving."

Veral absorbed that new human phrase. The human species was strange, but he was enjoying his mate's idiosyncrasies. Her turn of phrase was just one of the more amusing things that made every day a delight. He could imagine their half-human offspring carrying on such charming traits. His arms tightened protectively around her.

They would be free soon.

He attempted to make contact again with Kaylar, but received nothing but silence. He frowned at that but continued to make his way through the corridor with his mate secure in his arms. Kaylar was hard to kill, even more difficult than Veral. He would arrive.

26

Being carried made Terri feel like a burden, but knowing there was a reason for it was a relief, even if she didn't understand the explanation he had offered. She might not have the strength right now, but she peered over his right shoulder, her cheek nestled against his neck. She would be an extra set of eyes for her mate, to compensate as much as she could for the loss of his vibrissae. The shorn ends twitched against her uselessly, a reminder of the terrible pain and disorientation he was experiencing.

Veral had swung her on to his back and taken off down the hall. His balance was definitely off, and he seemed to turn his head frequently to the right to compensate for his blind spot.

"I'm watching on your right," she whispered in his ear. "Trust me. We'll work together to get through here."

He did not reply, but she didn't expect him to. Instead, he squeezed one of her thighs he had boosted up around his hips affectionately in acknowledgement.

"I swear, if I get out of this, I'm never going on a planet again. Filthy, dangerous places creeping with things that want to eat you. My ship, and even the most broken-down space station, would be preferable to this," Azan wheezed, squinting into the distance while maintaining her ground-eating pace. "No more fleeing from creatures trying to eat me. The only running I plan on doing from here on out is short bursts to evade law enforcement. Space is far more civilized."

Terri chuckled tiredly at the observation. She could just imagine the pirate holed up on one ship or another for the rest of her life, charting a new course the moment someone so much as whispered about having to land planetside.

Azan shot her a sidelong look. "What about you, little human? Are you sure the life of a salvager is right for you? There would be a place for you on my ship. Nice, cozy… minimal chance of being eaten."

Veral stiffened against Terri, and she rubbed her hand soothingly on the thick muscle of her male's arm. "I'm quite sure. I can't think of anywhere else I'd like to be other than my mate's side."

"Your species must possess a limited imagination," Azan retorted, laughing.

Terri shrugged and nestled closer to her mate, breathing in his warm scent. She wouldn't live in a cage, no matter how lovely. Anything less than being at her mate's side was unacceptable. Veral's threatening growl at the suggestion warmed her heart as she recognized the demonstration of her male's claim in response to the pirate's words. The territorial sound was as close to violence as Veral could get at that moment.

If Azan had been another male offering what could be perceived as a better, more comfortable, life, she wondered if he would have managed to control his reaction, injury be damned. Any worry she had that he would consider casting her aside when their relationship became too much trouble evaporated at that sound. Even after everything that had happened over the last several days, he was demonstrating—in as grand of a gesture as it got with him—that she was completely his.

"I'll be yours for as long as you want me," she whispered.

A purr rattled from him, his hands tightening around her legs. "Never would there be a time or place where I would not need my anastha, or lay my life and honor before you. You may be mine, but I am yours as well," he replied, the heartfelt lengthiness of his response surprising Terri.

Azan sighed. "You two are disgusting. How unlikely that your relationship survived this long intact. How is that, I wonder? Regardless, it was worth the attempt."

Veral snorted and shook his head. "You do not understand mating. It is not about what is pleasant in fortunate circumstances, but that which survives and is tempered by life. My anastha is the other half of me. She carries my heart and all of my future, pirate."

Azan directed a twisted grimace in his direction. "You are saying that because she is capable of carrying your offspring…"

"No," Veral interrupted, his voice sharp with anger as he cleared rubble that lay in their path. "Offspring are desired but are not the soul of a mating. She is my future not by what her body may issue but that her presence in my life provides a richer meaning by sharing my life with her. She is a light that brings greater clarity to my purpose. Darkness that descends upon us does not extinguish that light, but makes it that much clearer to see when that bond is focused upon rather than things that cannot be changed. She was made to be by my side, and the gods have seen fit to provide her with what she needed to accomplish this. Our experiences together, even the difficult ones, provide the tools."

"I did not realize that the Argurma were so romantic," Azan teased with a devilish smirk.

Veral snorted. "It is not romance. It is sound reasoning."

"So you say... How much longer until we get out of here? I have had all that I can stomach of this mated bliss."

Her reply was met with a loud chuff from Veral as he peered about. He veered to the left, his limber body practically gliding across the floor with predatory grace that Terri could feel shifting in his muscles.

"The exit is ahead. We will arrive in the main chamber of the wreckage in..."

A loud groan started above them as the entire ship shook, an odd blast shaking it violently, casting apart debris as it fell everywhere. Terri shouted as a large section of the roof began to cave in, the metal buckling as it slid downward at an angle toward them. It squealed and screeched, jumbled among the other sounds as the ship appeared to be tearing apart. She wasn't even sure she could isolate the sound from that part of the ceiling specifically from the death cries of the ship.

"Veral, the ceiling is collapsing to your right!" she shouted around the sudden pressure of her heart leaping to her throat.

In a lightning-fast response, he spun to the side just enough to see the falling sheets of metal before darting out of range with Azan trailing close behind them. The sounds of falling metal and more distant sliding stone filled the air with such a blast of noise that she was uncertain exactly how long the world fell around them as they raced against destruction. She was aware, however, as the dust settled, that everything in the corridor had changed.

Veral lifted his head, looking around...listening. Terri noted that the AI, whose voice had been garbled during the collapse as it issued barely audible commands to evacuate, made no further attempts to communicate. There was nothing but a yawning gulf of destruction all around them. Terri's eyes roved over it from where she was still perched overlooking Veral's shoulder, an uneasy shiver sliding over her skin as she could make out patches of dim sunlight filtering down.

They were now more exposed than they had been, and all that noise...

"I don't suppose that went unnoticed..." she murmured.

She jerked as one of the large bird-like creatures swept overhead, its wide wings filling the air over the gap in the ceiling as it squawked. She swallowed nervously, but tensed further as she noticed that Veral wasn't even looking at the animal. Instead, he was completely still, head turned to the left as his expression tightened.

"Wha—"

He shook his head in admonishment, bidding her to be silent as he shifted his weight on his feet. Azan turned in the same direction as she palmed her blaster.

"Experiment 302," he hissed as the ground quivered with a small vibration, and then another.

The creature emerged from the shadows slowly, languidly, as if it didn't have a care in the world, secure in the knowledge that its prey wouldn't be able to outrun it. Unlike the larger monsters, its body was smaller and lithe with six long, narrow legs supported by clawed paws. The fact that it was smaller wasn't much of a boon, however, since it was still twice as tall as Veral.

The creature looked like no animal that Terri was familiar with. Its face was sharply tapered, six eyes blinking at them, forming a half ring on its face as two pairs of ears flicked and moved. As it stared at them with glowing, blood red eyes, its rigid upper lip rose, revealing sharp teeth offset by four sets of deadly fangs. A sail-like fan of skin at the end of its tail opened and snapped closed again as it studied them. Its mouth opened wider as it snarled just as a long tongue uncoiled, whipping erratically as it vibrated in the air not unlike one of Veral's vibrissae. This, however, had a hollow, sucker-like tube at the end that made Terri's stomach heave with fear.

With slow, gliding steps, it moved closer, a low, trembling

whine drawing through its throat. The sound was not the pitiful noise made by Krono when he was denied something he enjoyed, but a whine pitched in such a way that it made the hair on her arms stand up. A chill ran through her as it ceaselessly filled the air with desperation.

It was a sound of starvation. The sound of deep-seated hunger.

Veral moved back, one of his hands dropping away from supporting her as he allowed his claws to slide out from his free hand. 302 crouched down further, its muscles coiling as it readied itself to spring. A gurgle rose in Terri's throat. Exhausted as she was, she couldn't even help her mate beat the creature back with her handy symbiont as she had before.

It crouched even lower, its belly nearly touching the floor. It sprang at them with a snarl, a sound of rage mixing with its keening cries of hunger. Terri tucked her face into Veral's neck, prepared to meet her end. A blinding light flickered behind her eyes just as a loud blast cut through the air. Screams of pain rang out, stopping after only a second. Jerking her head up, she stared in awe as the plumes of smoke disappeared, revealing a bubbling mass of the creature lying on the floor. A chuff of laughter left Veral.

"Plasma cannon, warrior class," he stated with no little pleasure just as a large mass dropped down in front of them.

The figure uncurled as he stood, revealing himself to be an Argurma male somehow even bigger than Veral. His face was broader, with a more sharply defined square jaw. His vibrissae practically stood straight out from his head in an enormous halo as he absorbed information on everything in the area. His expression was hard and foreboding despite the small smile that just barely turned up the edges of his mouth.

"Veral," he said, his glowing amethyst eyes narrowing.

"Kaylar," Veral returned in greeting, though he made no attempt to approach.

The male, Kaylar, tilted his head in acknowledgement before flicking his eyes to the remains of the experiment. "Is that it?"

"Yes," Veral replied. "The pirates in our company are dead, and that was the only land-mobile experiment within the remains of the ship, although I make no guarantee what that blast might have attracted from the outer areas."

The other male shrugged. "I required a quick entrance. I loaded the virus into the pirate ship and set my ship into auto-hover mode so that I could lower myself down to the wreckage. I did not expect to encounter flying beasts that attempted to chew on me midair. Blasting my way through the hull seemed to be an expedient solution to get away from them once I became bored with their games." His eyes flicked to Azan, who immediately held her hands up in reaction to his hard gaze. "What of the Blaithari?"

"An ally. She poses no threat."

"I see. And the coordinates?"

Veral nodded. What did their rescue have to do with coordinates? Terri stared in confusion at Veral as he initiated the data transfer. "Wait—what?"

The ghost of a smile widened on the male's face as he accepted the transfer and nodded in approval as he no doubt reviewed the information. "Your mate did not tell you? I am not surprised. It is in his nature to protect, whereas it is not in mine. Another flaw in his systems. You should know that the council is very interested in your species. That you are biologically compatible with Argurmas could have interesting implications when it comes to usefulness for organ harvesting and organic replacement tissue for our species, among other uses in testing. It is believed that a female would be preferable to keep for initial testing."

Terri's mouth dropped open, and she leaned back so she could adequately turn her head and stare at her mate in shock. "You didn't..."

"It was necessary. It was all that he would accept for his aid. He has the virus codes that are temporarily disabling the pirate ship orbiting the planet. It was the only way to save you," he growled.

Terri swallowed back her dismay and the many rebukes that had been ready to fly off the tip of her tongue. She hated that he gave up that information without even consulting her, but perhaps he had known that she wouldn't have agreed. He wouldn't sit back and let harm come to her. He would sacrifice anything for her.

She couldn't say that she wouldn't have done the same.

She leaned into him, worrying about the fate of the women she had left behind on Earth who wouldn't even know that anyone was coming after them.

"Interesting," Kaylar said quietly. "Even after your betrayal, she still cleaves to you."

She shot him an annoyed glare. "I'm not so stupid that I don't recognize he did it for me and our child. As much as I hate you right now for what you're about to do, I can't be angry at him for making that choice. I would have done the same for him."

A heavy brow rose in her direction, and he hummed thoughtfully to himself. "Interesting." He gave them a long, considering look before he shrugged and drew an enormous blaster from his back, leveling it on Veral. "I am truly in awe, cousin, that you have had the good fortune to find a worthy mate. Unfortunately, that doesn't change anything for you. I do believe it is time for you to surrender."

"Betrayal, Kaylar?"

One corner of the male's mouth pulled up in a genuine smile. "Business only. Truly, I will regret it, but when the council learned of where I was going, they commanded it. There is no keeping anything from them for long—as you should know."

Veral nodded and very slowly lowered Terri to her feet. His

fingers flexed as he glared at the male he called cousin. "You will understand if I insist that I must decline."

Kaylar's smile widened, and he chuffed again. "Of course, naturally! Not that I think it will do you much good when you have lost a quarter of your vibrissae. It is a good look for you, however," he said, with another laugh echoing around him.

Veral smiled in reply, his body loose as he faced off with the other male. Terri didn't even see the attack coming. Veral rushed from her side, his claws out as he struck out with fury at the Argurma before him. She choked in surprise even as everything within her prayed for victory.

27

*A*zan watched dispassionately as Veral charged the newcomer. She really did not have a stake in this personal disagreement, but a life debt would be difficult to settle if the male she owed was locked up or dissected somewhere. With the Argurma, it was difficult to judge what the punishment may be.

Besides, she liked Terri. Azan was still of the opinion that the little female would fare better with her, but she was not one to try to take choices away. In any case, she had taken the opportunity to intercept the coordinates. She could always find a small, soft human of her own. It would seem like bad manners to accept or steal such a fine gift without even attempting to even the field of engagement between the Argurmas.

Sighing, she pulled out her modified blaster. It had one grenade capsule implant left in the attachment. She hated to waste it, but she did not wish to appear ungrateful either. It was difficult dancing on the right side of morality. Absolutely disgusting.

She squinted at the males as they tore into each other, metal-enhanced claws slashing at each other. Raising one hand, she glanced down at her own simple claws with a pang of envy.

Perhaps once Veral straightened out the reason for being hunted down she could talk him into assisting her with acquiring the modification. He would have to be alive to do that.

Yes. That settles it.

Leaning down, she gently unwound Garswal's arms from around her shoulders and gave his arm a firm pat. He was a good kid. She would watch out for him.

"Stay here, and stay low," she whispered.

He nodded and ducked down behind the nearby pile of fallen rock. Azan nodded with approval before turning away to face the fray. Terri leaned heavily against a wall, her arm raised, the creepy symbiont flaring uselessly as she tried to work it beyond her available resources. The idea of tech that drew metals from blood so casually made her skin crawl, but she could not deny it was good defense for the human, so long as she did not exhaust herself.

Oh well. Azan to the rescue. She hoped no one got word of this.

Raising her blaster, she squinted at the males. Damned Argurma looked the same as far as she could tell. Where was the one with the damaged head whips... Ah, there he was. The other was her target. She pulled the trigger, the sound of the implant discharging a faint whistle. But he felt it when it implanted. The male jerked away from Veral, his body arching as he roared in agony.

That was the damned thing about the implants. They were designed to burrow deep into the body and attach to the bone. They could not be dug out. Even a medic would have a difficult time removing it without detonating it. A cold smile curled her lips as the male spun to her, his hand clutching his side. That had to hurt as it dug through all that tissue to attach to the spine. She was fairly certain that her aim had missed the vital organs.

A cold smile stretched wide across her face. "Now that I have your attention, I am afraid I cannot let you take my new... ah, friends. I have debts to repay, and it would be difficult for me to do that if I let you take them. That little sting you felt—ah, more than a sting I suppose—that was a grenade implant capsule. Oh, you *have* heard of them," she said with a small laugh as the shock broke through the impassive expression that the male bore. His face immediately shut down once more as he glared at her.

"What do you want, female?" he snarled.

That was unpleasant of him, but from her recent experiences, Argurma did not have good manners anyway.

"Simple. Return them to their ship, and then me to mine. I will give you the docking codes to align with my ship. Once I am aboard and am certain that my friends are safe, I will comm you the deactivation code."

"The council—"

"Not my problem. Consider this a small mercy. That male there is very protective of his female, and I fear what he might do to you or anyone you turn them over to if you are fortunate enough. Especially once that little human has recovered and that symbiont armor is operational again. None of you are going to enjoy that nasty little surprise. Take my word on that. If you even think of trying to kill me and take them anyway, I might remind you that without the code, the grenade will detonate in thirty-six galactic standard hours."

"I don't understand. If you had something like that all this time, why didn't you use it before now?" Terri asked in disbelief as she sagged against her mate. Once he had noted that Azan had the situation well in hand, he had returned to his mate, gathering her once more into his arms.

Azan gave the female a sharp grin. "Pirate ships are notoriously difficult to gain control of, and murdering the captain on his own ship is risky for one who attempts it. This worked out well in my favor. He died here going after his treasure, and I barely escaped, but returned to the crew to see them through the trials to come. I will be a hero. A far better scenario. Perhaps not exactly what I imagined, but worth the expenditure of the capsule."

Kaylar snarled and turned to glare at Veral. "I thought you said that this female posed no danger."

"I did not specify that she would not be dangerous to you," Veral said, his tone flat. "If you had not betrayed me, we would have returned her to her ship without incident."

"Very well. Seems no other options are available. The council will not be happy," Kaylar growled. To Azan's surprise his face suddenly relaxed, a smile tugging the hard line of his lips. "As your pirate friend says, however, not my problem. I will inform them of the situation and return to my previous assignment. Let us return to the surface of the ship. The disembarkation platform is waiting there. It is a dinix-class platform. It will fit us all easily with room to spare."

With a pleased smile, Azan returned her blaster to its holster. No more walking through jungles and hot bogs… She could not have planned it better!

28

Now that the matter between Kaylar and Veral seemed to be settled, and to her surprise and amusement neither male seemed to hold a grudge at all over the matter, Terri was able to relax and observe the interior of an Argurma warship. It wasn't as large as the salvager, but it was extremely comfortable. She settled at a table, practically groaning with relief at having an actual place to sit for the first time in days. All the tension and worry that had plagued her eased out of her, leaving only a bone-wearying exhaustion.

Azan flopped in the chair beside her and sighed, her eyes also on the males seated opposite them, pouring over holograms of star charts as the ship navigated toward where the salvager awaited. She had returned from one of the cabins where she had taken Garswal, after filling him with foods from Kaylar's replicator, so that he could sleep. The female rubbed her face and sighed mournfully.

"I can't believe we went through all that hell and came away with so little," she muttered. "All that gold… The finest metals I've ever seen. And the giant gems! No, instead I'm walking away with that stinky old robe covered in decomposition powder. You can keep that."

"I am certain that our client may purchase it. If not, I can find a buyer who will appreciate a rare item of antiquity," Veral interjected. "It may be the only thing that will even partially reimburse us for the expenses of this salvage."

Terri blinked and sat up, a smile flooding her face as excitement sent a burst of energy through her.

"That's not the only thing that will reimburse us," she said with a small laugh.

Everyone fell silent and watched as she grinned smugly and began unsealing the storage pouches on her armor. Each time her fingers slipped inside a pouch, she pulled at the ornate jewelry, gold chains, pouches of round gold coins that apparently were used before the credits system, and so many gems. Azan's gasp was the only sound that filled the room as everyone stared at the growing pile. It was a good thing that the storage pouches held a lot without it being noticeable, because even bursting full, none of the pirates had noticed any prominent bulges in her armor from her collection.

Finally, she sat the last gem on the table, a blood red stone nearly the size of her hand, and sighed happily. "I do think that this should take care of it."

"You found all of this without going inside the treasury?" Azan asked in disbelief.

"Yes, seems like the prince enjoyed surrounding himself with wealth in a very real sense," Terri replied.

Azan whistled between her teeth as Veral handed Terri a bag. She methodically began to swipe the treasure from the table into the sack. She would find a better place to store it once they returned to their ship. She left aside an ornate necklace set with glittering gems for Azan. It only seemed fair, though it pricked at her to part with something that would supply them for an even longer period. She shook it off and scraped the rest inside.

Turning to the pirate, she pushed the necklace toward her over the table. "It's only fair that you take something after everything down there. You kept me safe and helped us escape the planet."

Azan fingered it, a small smile on her lips. "I should say that I could not take this, but I have been a pirate too long and am greedy by nature. So I accept." She swept the necklace easily over her neck, her smile widening as she sat back in her chair. "A satisfactory exchange."

"Do I get nothing?" Kaylar asked crossly.

Terri scowled. "You got coordinates and still tried to double-cross us. I think walking out alive is reward enough."

The male shook his head, an approving look lighting his eyes as he glanced toward Veral. "I see why you have kept her as your mate. She is stronger than she appears."

Veral's eyes met hers, his lips curving with affection. "She is everything."

EPILOGUE

It took them little effort to capture the pirate who'd been left on their ship. Since he had taken good care of Krono despite his attempts to chew and claw his way through the door, Veral decided to be merciful, with little urging from Terri. The Blaithari, a younger male among the crew, had no problem swearing loyalty to Azan. Kaylar had long since left with both pirates, leaving Veral and Terri to make preparations to leave the planet far behind them.

She wasn't sorry to see the planet shrinking in the distance as their ship left the stratosphere. She couldn't help the edge of worry as they drew up parallel to the pirate ship, but as promised, the pirate ship remained inactive, Kaylar's ship still attached to it. She wondered how much success Azan was having with the crew.

She smiled with a sudden bubble of mirth. Azan could be quite persuasive when she wanted to be.

The viewscreen flickered with the coordinates as Veral input them through his link. As soon as they locked, the ship turned away from the planet, the engines firing into primary drive.

Terri returned her attention to placing the last of the jewels in the storage case that Veral brought out for her. Krono's heavy head rested on her feet as she worked.

She frowned as she scraped the bottom of the empty bag. Something was missing. What happened to the blood red jewel? She began to pat her storage compartments in her armor. Maybe she had placed it in there by mistake.

A chime sounded through the ship, startling her from her task.

"Incoming transmission from the pirate ship… *Lady's Glory*," he added, a quizzical note to his voice.

Terri chuckled. "See? I told you that ships have names. It sure didn't take Azan long to place her own brand on it."

"So it seems," Veral replied as he put the message through.

Azan's grinning face filled the viewscreen a moment later.

"I see that you are well on your way. You will be pleased to note that I have successfully taken captainship of *Lady's Glory* and your Kaylar is disembarking. I wanted to thank you again and wish you safe journeys."

"What of Garswal?"

A fond look came over the pirate. "Ah, him. There is hope for that small male, and I find I cannot bear to part with him, so he will remain at my side. I will care for him and teach him to be a better male than his sire and most of the males on this ship. Do not worry for him."

"I am relieved to hear it. Safe journeys to you as well," Terri returned. "Try not to get into too much trouble."

"Only if the price is right and the moment opportune," Azan returned with a chuckle. "But only after the ship has had some overhauls. Which reminds me, thank you for your contribution to the efforts."

"Contribution…?" Terri asked, a frown of confusion wrinkling her brow. Veral chuffed with laughter, but she didn't get it.

Azan tossed a large, brilliant red gemstone in her hand. "I am afraid I could not let you leave with it—not when the ship requires considerable work."

Terri's mouth dropped open. She hadn't even seen the pirate take it. "Wait one damn minute…"

"Sorry, sweet little human. I do like you, but I am still a pirate, after all. Farewell!" Azan gave her a small salute as the screen blipped off.

In the viewscreen, she watched as the pirate ship's engines flared to life, the ship retreating as Kaylar's ship moved in a different direction, on his own way to Earth.

Terri shook her head, her shock fading into amusement. Sitting back in her chair, she locked the chest and shrugged. "I guess I should have expected that. Maybe I am still a naïve, weak human."

"Indeed, you should have expected nothing less," her mate replied, his eyes shining at her with warmth. Slowly, he got up from his chair and walked over, stopping in front of her. Leaning down, he plucked the box from her lap and set it aside as he drew her to her feet in front of him. "But you are anything but weak. You have shown great strength and an ability to protect yourself, especially now armed with a symbiont that will ensure your protection. Even without it, I should have known that you would be able to face anything that the cosmos sets before you. I admire and adore you. I was wrongly overprotective."

"You see that, finally, do you?" she asked with a small smile, her body leaning into his. "For the record, I actually like that you're protective and territorial. Just do it with me at your side rather than hidden away like I'm too fragile to trust to be with you."

"I shall. We are united in this together, for the rest of our span of life."

"Nothing sounds better to me. And what of your people? We

got rid of Kaylar easily enough. What if they send someone we can't handle?"

Veral's expression hardened. "The council would be unwise to send anyone else, but if they do, then we will take the fight to them. Until that happens, however, we will continue to just live."

"That doesn't sound highly logical," she teased.

"Perhaps not, but I have discovered that life with a human is not always logical... and yet it is surprisingly full and rewarding. This is a life I never could have imagined, but one I will never let go." His breath feathered against her skin, and as the final words left him, he lifted her into his arms and carried her from the bridge.

Life wasn't like one of the storybooks, but as he carried her to their room, Terri decided she was looking forward to her own sort of happily ever after.

OTHER WORKS BY S.J. SANDERS

The Mate Index
First Contact
The VaDorok
Hearts of Indesh (Valentine Novella)
The Edoka's Destiny
The Vori's Mate
Eliza's Miracle (Novella)
A Kiss on Kaidava
The Vori's Secret
A Mate for Oigr (Halloween Novella)
Heart of the Agraak
A Gift for Medif
The Arobi's Queen
Teril's Fire (coming soon)

Monsterly Yours
The Orc Wife
The Troll Bride
The Accidental Werewolf's Mate
Love Blooms for the Pixie Queen (coming soon)
The Unicorn's Mare (coming Dec 2020)

Sci-Fi Fairytales
Red: A Dystopian World Alien Romance

The Sirein: (coming soon)

Ragoru Beginnings Romance

White: Emala's Story

Huntress

Dark Spirits

Havoc of Souls

The Mirror (also part of Mischief Matchmakers)

Forest of Spirits

Desert of the Vanished (coming soon)

Shadowed Dreams Erotica

The Lantern

Serpent of the Abyss

The Mintars

Librarian and the Beast

The Atlavans

The Darvel Exploratory Systems

Classified Planet: Turongal

Argurma Salvager

Broken Earth

Pirate's Gold

ABOUT THE AUTHOR

S.J. Sanders is a writer of Science Fiction and Fantasy Romance. With a love of all things alien and monster she is fascinated with concepts of far off worlds, as well as the lore and legends of various cultures. When not writing, she loves reading, sculpting, painting and travel (especially to exotic destinations). Although born and raised in Alaska, she currently as a resident of Florida with her family, her maine coon, Bella, and pet bearded dragon, Lex.

Readers can follow her on Facebook

https://www.facebook.com/authorsjsanders

Or join her Facebook group S.J. Sanders Unusual Playhouse

https://www.facebook.com/groups/361374411254067/

Newsletter:

https://mailchi.mp/7144ec4ca0e4/sjsandersromance

Website:
   https://sjsandersromance.wordpress.com/

Printed in Great Britain
by Amazon